Garden Girls Cozy Mystery Series Book 9

Hope Callaghan

http://hopecallaghan.com
Copyright © 2015
All rights reserved.

This book is a work of fiction. Although places mentioned may be real, the characters, names and incidents and all other details are products of the author's imagination and are fictitious. Any resemblance to actual events or actual persons, living or dead is purely coincidental.

No part of this publication may be copied, reproduced in any format, by any means, electronic or otherwise, without prior consent from the copyright owner and publisher of this book. The only exception is brief quotations in printed reviews.

Visit my website for new releases and special offers: hopecallaghan.com

Thank you, Peggy Hyndman, for taking the time to preview *Fall Girl,* for the sharp eyes that catch my mistakes.

TABLE OF CONTENTS

Chapter 1

Chapter 2

Chapter 3

Chapter 4

Chapter 5

Chapter 6

Chapter 7

Chapter 8

Chapter 9

Chapter 10

Chapter 11

Chapter 12

Chapter 13

Chapter 14

Chapter 15

Chapter 16

Chapter 17

Chapter 18

Chapter 19

Chapter 20

FREE Books and More!

Margaret's Magnificent Meatloaf

Easy Cheesy Hash Brown Casserole

About The Author

Chapter 1

Gloria Rutherford peered into the mirror that hung over the buffet table in her dining room. She turned her head from side to side, as she surveyed the camouflage face paint. "Lucy! I look like I'm ready to crawl through the trenches of the back 40!"

Gloria had to wonder how in the world she had ever let her best friend, Lucy, talk her into deer hunting in the first place. She vaguely remembered agreeing to think about it. Next thing she knew, Lucy was on her doorstep with camo gear, face paint and a hunting rifle that weighed almost as much as she did.

"I'm hot." Gloria pulled on the collar of her jacket as a trickle of perspiration inched down her back.

"You don't want the deer to see you," Lucy patiently explained. She knew that once Gloria got used to the idea that she was going to try hunting, at least once, she would settle down.

Lucy patted her jacket pocket to make sure she still had the deer lure. If Gloria was putting up this kind of fuss over the face paint, she wondered how she would react when she got a whiff of the deer lure...

Lucy knew she had to take baby steps with the whole hunting thing. Once Gloria got accustomed to the rifle, the camo gear and the face paint, she would slip in the deer lure.

Maybe she should wait until they were out in the woods to spring that one on her friend.

The girls trudged through the kitchen as they made their way out onto the back porch.

Mally, Gloria's springer spaniel, met them at the door. "Sorry girl," Gloria reached down and patted her head. "You can't go this time."

Visions of poor Mally accidentally getting shot filled Gloria's head. It wasn't that Gloria thought she would shoot her, or even Lucy, but there would be other hunters out in the fields and Mally liked to wander off.

They stepped out onto the porch and into the cool morning air. It was still early and the first rays of daylight peeked over the top of the barn across the street.

Lucy's eyes shifted to the old farmhouse across the road. Crime scene vans and police cars filled the drive. "What's going on over there?"

Gloria frowned. She had noticed the same vehicles across the street when she'd come home the night before. Her plan was to run over there this morning to try to find out what had happened but all that was forgotten when Lucy arrived on her doorstep with the hunting gear.

Gloria's husband, James, and his family had owned the old farmhouse across the road for decades.

James' brother had lived in the house for years until one day he up and moved out. After he moved, the siblings decided to sell the house. A local farmer bought the property, lock, stock and barrel solely for the farmland. The house had stood vacant for many years.

A young couple had recently purchased the home and were in the midst of completing some much-needed major renovations before they moved in.

"I have no idea," Gloria replied. "The crime scene van was there last night."

Judging by the yellow police tape that wound around the trees and the front porch, Gloria could only guess that someone had died. She hoped it wasn't the Fowlers, the nice young couple who had purchased the place.

Gloria pulled the collar of her jacket around the nape of her neck as a brisk November gust of wind whipped strands of hair across her face. She stepped onto the sidewalk and started down the drive. There was only one way to find out what was going on.

Lucy picked up the pace and fell into step with Gloria. She knew her friend well enough to know that her curiosity had gotten the best of her.

Gloria looked both ways and darted across the road. She hoped that Officer Nelson, or better yet, Gloria's fiancé, Paul, was on the scene and that they would fill her in on what had happened.

Her heart sank when two investigators stepped out onto the narrow front porch. One looked vaguely familiar. She had never seen the other one before.

Gloria came to a halt at the bottom of the steps. "Hello. I'm Gloria Rutherford. I live across the street and was wondering what was going on."

The officer on the left, a burly man with a solemn expression, stepped forward. "Yes, ma'am. It appears there was a homicide. We are in the midst of a preliminary investigation."

He pulled a notepad from his front pocket, along with an ink pen. He flipped the lid of the pad. "You said you live across the street?"

Gloria nodded. "Yes. I'm Gloria Rutherford." She pointed toward the house. "The person who was found...dead. W-was it one of the new owners?"

The officer shifted his gaze and studied Gloria. "We are not releasing information about the victim at this time."

He went on. "We...err...aren't able to make a positive ID, yet. That may take some time. It doesn't appear to be the current owners."

Gloria wasn't sure if she should feel relieved.

"Can you at least tell us if you think it's a local resident?" Lucy piped up. The Town of Belhaven, where both Gloria and Lucy lived, was small. Everyone knew everyone else. If the victim was a local, there was a good chance the girls would know who it was.

"Sorry ma'am. I can't give out any other information." He turned back to Gloria and began to ask her if she'd seen anything unusual. Then he asked her where she'd been the night before.

"I can vouch for her," Lucy defended. "She was at a party. In fact, several others can vouch for her, too!"

That was true. The girls had just celebrated Gloria's recent windfall, along with their other close friends: Ruth, Margaret, Dot and Andrea.

The cop shifted his stance and rubbed his jaw thoughtfully. "She was with you all night?"

Gloria swallowed hard. Did the officer think she was somehow involved? Surely, they wouldn't try to pin a murder on an innocent woman if they couldn't find the killer!

The officer asked a few more questions and Gloria had a hunch he was trying to incriminate her. He flipped the pad of paper shut and shoved it in his front pocket. "My name is Officer Fred Burnett. I have your information and will be in touch with you in the next day or so."

With the sweep of his hand, he dismissed the women, turned on his heel and walked back inside the house.

"What a jerk," Lucy hissed. She patted Gloria's arm. "Don't worry about it, Gloria. All of us girls can vouch for you!"

The girls strode across the road as they made their way back to Gloria's farm. Gloria wasn't in the mood to hunt now. Not that she had been in the first place but now she wanted to go even less.

The corners of her lips turned down as she stalked to the backyard.

"Hunting will take your mind off this whole thing," Lucy promised her. "Maybe after we're out of the woods, we can run into town to see if Dot has heard anything." Dot was one of the girls' close friends. She owned Dot's Restaurant, the only restaurant in the small Town of Belhaven.

"Good idea," Gloria agreed.

The walk helped clear Gloria's head and by the time they reached the deer stand at the edge of the woods, she had almost forgotten about the entire incident.

Gloria owned more property than Lucy did and she had allowed her friend to build her tree stand on the edge of her favorite wooded area near the back.

It was not far from the spot where Gloria and Mally often came to spend quiet time. Gloria visited the special place when she needed to be alone.

Lucy stopped abruptly in front of a large oak tree. "We're here."

Gloria's eyes traveled up the tree, past the crude, wooden steps Lucy had constructed, to a small platform a good fifteen feet up in the air. "We...we're going to go up there?"

"Yep." Lucy grasped the first rung. "Trust me. It's not so bad once you get up there." Lucy scampered up the tree. When she got to the top, she turned around and looked down at Gloria. "C'mon."

Gloria sucked in a breath. "I don't know about this." She placed both hands on the first rung and began to climb. Her heavy farm boots scraped roughly against the tree bark as she ascended the rungs. The rungs were sturdy and even she was surprised at how easy it was to navigate.

Gloria took a quick glance at the ground below. Maybe now she could venture into the tree fort her grandsons had built in her front yard. When she reached the top, she crawled onto the platform and plopped down on her rear. "That wasn't so bad."

"See?" Lucy said. "I told you." She settled in next to Gloria, reached into her pocket and pulled out the small plastic container of deer lure. She flipped the top and squeezed a small amount into the palm of her hand.

The overpowering smell of urine filled the air and Gloria's nose. She gasped for fresh air as she frantically waved her hand across her face. "Good heavens. What in the world…"

Lucy calmly rubbed her hands together and then wiped the palms of her hands on the sleeves of her hunting jacket. "It's deer lure. It masks the human scent so the deer won't know that we're here," she explained.

Lucy poured another dose into her hand and began to wipe it on Gloria's pant legs.

Gloria jerked her leg back. "Stop! That smell makes me want to throw up!" She pushed Lucy's hand away.

Lucy stopped wiping. "Okay." She lowered her head and slowly closed the lid of the lure. Her expression was so crestfallen that Gloria felt bad. She had hurt Lucy's feelings. "Okay. Wipe away!" she groaned.

The smile returned and Lucy quickly began swiping the stinky substance on Gloria's jacket in an attempt to finish before Gloria had time to change her mind.

When she finished, she closed the lid on the bottle and slipped it back inside her jacket.

"Now what?" Gloria asked.

"We wait," Lucy said.

***

The girls sat as quiet as church mice. The woods were peaceful. The only sound was an occasional gunshot off in the distance. After the third time of hearing gunshots, Lucy set her rifle on the wooden deck and dropped her chin in her hands. "I wish that was me."

Gloria didn't. She had only come on this merry little hunting excursion for Lucy's sake. On top of that, she had no idea how the two of them would manage to drag a deer from the woods if Lucy did shoot one.

They stayed in the same spot for what seemed like eternity, although according to Gloria's watch, it had only been a couple hours.

Gloria shifted onto her knees and groaned. They hadn't seen hide nor hair of a deer.

Lucy could see that Gloria had reached her limit. "Wanna head back?"

Gloria opened her mouth to reply when Lucy whacked her in the arm. "Wait! There's a buck!"

Lucy lifted her rifle. She stuck the butt of the gun on her shoulder and pointed the barrel at the buck, which lifted his head and looked around.

Gloria braced herself for the gunshot but dared not make a move lest she scare the deer.

"Pow!"

Lucy fired off a shot and then lowered the rifle as she tilted her head forward. "Darn! I missed! That was a five point buck!" she sighed.

"We can stay a little longer," Gloria relaxed her body, her ears still ringing from the sound of the gun firing. She hadn't realized how much of a fanatic her friend was over deer hunting. Maybe if she stayed long enough, she would be off the hook for the next time.

"Nah!" Lucy flipped the safety lever in place and slipped the gun into the carrying case. "It's a lost cause. Now that I fired a shot, all the deer in the area will be spooked. I won't get another shot in today."

Gloria followed her friend out of the tree. When she reached the bottom rung, she hopped onto the ground. "Well, that was interesting." She lifted the sleeve of her jacket and sniffed the surface. "Pee-yew!" If anything, the smell had intensified.

"Don't worry. I'll take the jacket home and store it in the shed for next time." The jacket belonged to Lucy and Gloria was relieved she wouldn't have to worry about getting the stinky smell out.

The girls wandered out of the woods and made their way down the strip of grass that ran between the empty farm fields as they walked back to Gloria's place.

When they reached the driveway, Lucy loaded the stinky garments into the back of her jeep. "Do you still want to go to Dot's place?"

Gloria glanced across the street. All was quiet. The police vehicles were gone and the drive was empty. "Yeah. If you don't mind."

"Sure." Lucy climbed into the jeep and rolled down the window. "Stop by my place when you're ready and we can ride together."

Gloria waved at Lucy, who stopped at the end of the drive and then pulled out onto the road.

She could see Mally's head peeking through the glass pane of the door as she stepped onto the porch. She opened the porch door and Mally sprinted out.

Gloria stood on the porch and waited for her pooch to stretch her legs. She gazed across the street and shivered. The young couple who had bought the house had been there just the other day. That meant that someone had gone into that house and either killed someone or left a body in the last couple of days.

What were the chances that now that the house was in the midst of renovation, someone decided to use it to hide a body?

Gloria's blood chilled. Maybe the body had been inside for a long time, undiscovered until workers began renovation.

"C'mon girl." Mally and Gloria stepped inside the house. Gloria shut the door, clicked the deadbolt in place and then pulled on it, just to make sure it locked.

She walked to the bedroom, grabbed a pink sweater and pair of blue jeans and headed for the shower. While the water warmed, Gloria peeled off her sweaty flannel shirt and bib overalls, and climbed into the shower. Although she hadn't gotten "dirty" from hunting, she could still smell the lingering odor of deer urine.

After Gloria was squeaky clean, she headed out the door and climbed into Annabelle, her 1989 Mercury Grand Marquis.

When she got to Lucy's place, she pulled her car in behind Lucy's jeep, which was parked in the drive. She grabbed the handle of the door to open it when Lucy emerged from the house and darted down the steps.

Lucy slid into the passenger seat and reached for the seat belt. "I have a new strategy for next time we go hunting," she exclaimed excitedly.

Gloria grimaced. "What's that?"

Lucy smiled slyly. "It's a surprise."

Gloria rolled her eyes. She could hardly wait. "Does it involve baiting the deer with sweets?" Lucy was notorious for her sweet tooth and although Lucy ate excessive amounts of sugary goodies, she never seemed to gain an ounce.

Gloria pulled Annabelle into an empty spot in front of the restaurant. It was still early for the lunch crowd and they easily found a table near the back.

Dot darted over to the table. She set a Diet Coke in front of Gloria and a regular Coke in front of Lucy. "How did the hunting go? Did you get your deer?"

"Nope." Gloria pulled the wrapper off her straw and slid it into her drink. "But it wasn't because the deer knew we were there. Lucy smeared enough deer lure on us to last a month."

Lucy shot her friend a dark look. "I did not. I only put a little on you," she argued.

Dot stuck the empty tray under her arm. "I heard they found a body in that old house across the street from your place."

Gloria wiped at a speck on the tabletop. She took a deep breath and nodded. "That's why we're here. Well, one of the reasons. Have you heard anything?"

Dot shook her head. "Officer Nelson was in here earlier. When I tried to pump him for information, he clammed up. He said we'd find out soon enough."

"Let me guess. You're talking about the body found in the house across the street from Gloria's." Ruth, the girls' friend who was also head postmaster at Belhaven post office, had come up behind them.

Gloria turned her head. "Yeah. We wondered if maybe Dot had heard anything."

Now that Gloria thought about it, if anyone had insider information, it would be Ruth. Ruth was always one of the first to hear the scuttlebutt around town.

Ruth unzipped her jacket, slipped her arms out of the sleeves and hung it on the back of the chair before sliding into an empty seat. She eyed Lucy uneasily and then turned to Gloria. "Yeah. A few people were in this morning talking about it."

"And?" Lucy leaned forward.

Ruth dropped her eyes, a sure sign that what she was about to say was going to be unpleasant.

"Judith Arnett said she heard it was Bill Volk."

Chapter 2

Gloria's heart plummeted. Her eyes shifted to Lucy, who had turned as white as a ghost.

Dot gasped.

Bill Volk was Lucy's ex-boyfriend. They had dated for over a year and broken up just a few months earlier. The breakup hadn't been amicable but then it hadn't been nasty, either. Uncomfortable was the word Lucy used to describe the breakup.

Gloria reached out and squeezed Lucy's hand. "We don't know for sure."

She turned to Ruth. "Right? I mean, it's just a rumor."

Ruth nodded. "That's just the word on the street, Lucy. They found some identification on the body that may be Bill's. At least that's the gossip."

Lucy's face went blank. She started to stand and then sat back down. "Maybe I should try to call Bill."

She reached for her cellphone, switched it to on and peered at the screen. Her eyes widened in disbelief. "He...it looks like Bill tried to call me yesterday but he didn't leave a message!"

Lucy pressed the call button and placed the phone against her ear.

The girls held their breath and waited, praying that Bill would pick up.

Tears welled in the back of her eyes as she disconnected the line. "There was no answer."

"Maybe you should leave a message," Dot suggested.

Lucy set the phone on the table. "And say what? 'Hey, I heard you were dead. Can you call me back?'"

She reached for the phone and dialed his number a second time. "Hello Bill. Lucy here. Can you please give me a call when you get a chance? Thanks."

Dot headed to the kitchen to grab a cup of coffee for Ruth. The trio sat in uncomfortable silence.

Gloria had a sudden thought. "Maybe you should try calling his store." Bill owned a small sporting goods store in the nearby Town of Green Springs.

"Good idea." For the third time, Lucy picked up her cell phone. "I'm not sure if I still have his work number programmed in my phone." She scrolled through the screen. "Yep. Here it is." She pressed the "call" button and put the phone to her ear.

The girls waited silently for someone to answer the other end of the line.

"Yes. This is Lucy. Lucy Carlson. Oh hey, Eric. I was wondering if Bill was around."

Gloria sucked in a breath.

Lucy listened silently for several moments. "No. No. I had no idea." She lowered her head into the palm of her hand. "I-I can't believe it. Okay. Thanks."

Lucy disconnected the line and looked up, her eyes brimming with unshed tears. "Bill's brother Randy just came into the store to tell the employees. Police think the body they found in the house across from Gloria's place was Bill."

A tear trickled down Lucy's cheek.

Gloria hopped out of her chair and rushed to her friend's side. She put an arm around her shoulder.

"I'm so sorry Lucy." She didn't know what else to say. The other girls: Ruth and Dot gathered around her as they tried to comfort their friend.

"Let's go to the back," Dot urged. She led the way and the girls headed to the kitchen.

Ray, Dot's husband, stood in front of the fryer. "The food couldn't have been that bad," he joked when he saw the look on the girls' faces.

Dot stood next to her husband. "Bill Volk's body was found in the house across the street from Gloria."

Ray set the fryer basket in the holder. He wiped his hands on the front of his apron. "How do you know?"

Dot explained what Lucy had just found out. "We don't know any details. The only thing we know is police are saying it was his body they found."

"You don't think Lucy would be a suspect..." He turned to Lucy.

The thought hadn't occurred to Gloria - or Lucy for that matter. Would Lucy be a suspect? Their break up hadn't been that long ago.

Gloria had heard that Bill already had a new girlfriend. Lucy had moved on and was dating Max Field, a man Gloria and she had met when they were investigating the disappearance of Milton Tilton, a resident of nearby Dreamwood Retirement Community.

"We could both be suspects." Lucy frowned at Gloria.

It was true. Gloria suspected she was already on police radar due to her proximity to the location of where the body had been found. Lucy would be a suspect as a disgruntled ex...with a penchant for guns and blowing stuff up.

"We don't know how he died," Gloria pointed out. Paul might know. The investigators the girls met earlier had been from neighboring Kensington County but the two police departments often crossed paths and many of the officers and investigators knew one another.

"Let me ask Paul."

The girls headed out the back door and over to the picnic table. Dot brought out several bowls of chili and the girls ate their food in silence.

Ray popped his head out the screen door. "Margaret just walked in." Margaret was one of the Garden Girls and another close friend.

"Send her back," Dot told him.

Seconds later, Margaret emerged from the restaurant. She studied her friends' faces. "Looks like you heard." She settled onto the bench seat directly across from Gloria.

"Yeah. Can you believe it?" Ruth shook her head.

Margaret folded her arms on the table. "I was gonna tell you that Don had stopped by Bill's store to pick up some golf balls first thing this morning. One of the employees told him they had found the owner shot to death in an abandoned house."

***

"This is getting worse by the minute," Lucy whispered. "What if they think I killed him?" She remembered the phone call Bill had made to her the day before. Had he wanted to tell her something, that he suspected someone was after him?

"Especially since Bill tried to call you," Gloria grimaced. "But Bill owned a sporting goods store and they sold guns," she added.

She glanced at Margaret. "I wonder if Bill's new girlfriend likes guns."

Gloria had to believe the woman did. Bill was a gung-ho outdoor enthusiast and had gotten Lucy interested in all kinds of new activities. It had been one of the reasons for the break up.

Bill planned for Lucy to go hunting with him and when she told him she wanted to spend time with her friends, he told her she could spend all the time she wanted with them. That argument had been the beginning of the end of their relationship.

Dot stacked the empty chili bowls while Gloria picked up the dirty spoons.

Margaret patted Lucy on the back. "I'm sorry Lucy. I can just imagine how hard this must be."

"I-I'll be fine," Lucy reassured her friends.

Gloria opted to stick to the alley as they made their way back to the car.

When they were safely inside the car, Gloria turned to her friend. "Do you wanna come spend the night at my house?" She was concerned about Lucy staying alone.

Lucy shook her head. "No. Jasper is home waiting for me." Jasper was the dog Lucy had recently adopted during Gloria's investigation at a local puppy mill. "Plus, Max is going to stop by later."

Gloria backed the car out of the parking spot and onto Main Street. She shifted the car into drive. "I need to stop by Andrea's place to find out Alice's plan to help the puppies."

Gloria had recently sold some valuable coins. She had promised to use some of the money she had gotten from the sale of the coins to turn a puppy mill they had stumbled upon into a training center for dogs. The plan was to train the dogs and then sell or donate them to those with special medical needs.

Alice and Andrea had assured Gloria that with proper training, the Acosta family, who owned the dogs, could turn it around and into something special.

"We can go now," Lucy said.

Gloria glanced down at the clock on her dashboard. "If you don't mind."

Andrea's newly remodeled mini mansion was near Lake Terrace and just blocks from downtown.

Gloria turned into Andrea's drive and parked behind her young friend's pick-up truck. Brian, Andrea's boyfriend, was also there.

Brian was Brian Sellers, the owner of Nails and Knobs Hardware store. He also owned several other small businesses in Belhaven, including a grocery store and pharmacy.

Andrea and Brian had been dating for quite a while now and Gloria wondered if someday soon Brian might pop the question to Andrea. Gloria was dying to ask but didn't want to seem nosy. She also didn't want to put poor Brian on the spot.

If truth be told, it was none of her business.

The girls climbed out of the car and made their way to the front door.

Gloria grasped the lion's head doorknocker and rapped sharply.

Minutes later, the door swung open and Alice, Andrea's former housekeeper and current housemate, greeted them. "Oh Miss Gloria!" she clapped her hands. "Andrea and I wondered if you forgot about us."

Gloria's eyes slid to Lucy, who stood next to her. "I got a little sidetracked earlier. I hope it's not too late to talk."

Alice reached for Gloria's hand and pulled her inside. "No! No. I spoke with Mr. Acosta today. He is still excited about our idea of turning his dog kennel into a training center."

The girls followed Alice down a small hall and into the library. "Miss Andrea and Brian are in here." She waved them into the warm, inviting room and then followed them in.

Andrea was sitting at a small desk in the corner. Brian was standing next to her. She quickly lowered the lid on the computer, which made Gloria instantly suspicious. Andrea reminded Gloria of one of her own children when they tried to hide something.

She took a step closer. "What are you doing dear?" she asked.

"Oh...just working on Thanksgiving and some minor details for your upcoming wedding," Andrea told her.

Gloria nodded. She certainly had her plate full. Thanksgiving would be the quietest affair. Gloria had invited her daughter, Jill, and Jill's family, along with Paul and his two children.

Christmas, on the other hand, was going to be the humdinger. Not only would all of Gloria's children be in town for the holiday, Gloria and her boyfriend, Paul Kennedy, planned to marry.

Andrea waved to the large, wingback leather chairs. "Have a seat."

Gloria slid into the seat closest to Andrea. She crossed her legs and leaned back in the chair. "Do you still want to visit the Acostas tomorrow?"

Andrea tucked a strand of blonde hair behind her ear. "Yes! Alice is driving me nuts."

"Good. Come by the house tomorrow morning and we'll ride together." Gloria turned to Lucy. "You can come, too."

Lucy wasn't paying any attention to the conversation. Her mind was a million miles away as she stared out through the library window at the backyard. "What? I'm sorry Gloria. I missed what you said."

"I said you can visit the puppy place with us, too."

Lucy frowned. "No. I think I'm going to hang around the house tomorrow."

She turned to Andrea. "I just found out that my ex-boyfriend, Bill's, body was found in the house across the street from Gloria."

Andrea's hand flew to her mouth. "Oh my gosh!" Andrea had met Bill right after she moved to Belhaven. She knew that Bill wasn't one of Gloria's favorite people and that Lucy and Bill's relationship had ended not long ago. "That's the first I've heard."

Andrea had had to deal with her own share of deaths, including the death of her husband, Daniel.

"That place has been vacant as long as I've lived in Belhaven," Andrea remarked.

Gloria shifted in her chair. "A young couple just bought the place and started to fix it up."

In the back of Gloria's mind, she had to wonder if whoever had killed Bill Volk had intentionally set out to frame Gloria. If that was the case, they were succeeding. It would only be a matter of time before police tied Bill to Lucy and then in a roundabout way, to Gloria.

Lucy must have thought the same thing. She slowly turned to Gloria. "You don't think someone killed Bill and left his body in the house across the street to frame you..."

That was exactly what Gloria thought. Someone had it in for Gloria, or Lucy. "As soon as I get back home, I'm going to call Paul to see what he knows." She slid out of the chair and rose to her feet. "I should get back. Mally and Puddles will be wondering what happened to me."

Andrea and Brian walked the girls to the front door.

Gloria shifted her purse on her shoulder. She glanced at Lucy. Neither she nor Lucy had ever been the focus of an investigation. "We need to do a little snooping around, starting with Bill's business."

The girls rode in silence as they headed to Lucy's place.

Gloria pulled into Lucy's drive, shifted the car into park and turned to her friend. "You gonna be okay?"

Lucy reached for the door handle and nodded. "Yeah. I don't think it has sunk in yet," she admitted. "Max will be here soon."

Gloria suspected that Lucy was still in shock. She made a mental note to call her later, before she went to bed that night.

She backed out of the drive and eased Annabelle onto the road. Shadows from the trees crept across the two-lane road. It would be dark soon and she would be glad to be home.

Gloria no longer cared to drive on the roads after dark. It was hard for her to judge distance. Not only that, but a freezing drizzle coated the roads making them a little slippery.

She breathed a sigh of relief when she pulled into her drive and parked the car in the garage. Her eyes wandered to the house across the street. It was dark, empty and looked sinister. The only light was Gloria's mercury light on the other side of the barn.

Gloria picked up the pace as she headed up the steps to the back porch. Someone - a killer - had been only yards away from her own front door.

She let Mally out for a brief run and then quickly brought her back in. She would need to be on alert until police apprehended the murderer.

Gloria dropped her purse on the chair and pulled her cell phone out. She dialed Paul's cell phone number and he picked up on the first ring. "I've been wondering when you were going to call," he said.

Gloria stepped over to the kitchen window, lifted the blind and peeked out. "I guess you heard."

Gloria could envision Paul rubbing his temples as he talked to his fiancé, who had a penchant for getting caught smack dab in the middle of some doozy investigations. "Fred Burnett, Kensington County's lead investigator, called a short time ago. Somehow, he found out that my soon-to-be bride lives right across the street from a crime scene."

"And?" Gloria asked.

"He was snooping around, asking vague questions about you."

Gloria's heart sank. She knew that there was now a bullseye on her back, and that someone was trying to frame her. She thought about Lucy. "You know that the deceased was Bill Volk, Lucy's ex-boyfriend."

There was a long silence on the other end of the line. "No. I heard the name but didn't put the two together." Long sigh. "This doesn't look good," he said.

After they hung up, Gloria made her way into the dining room. Puddles, Gloria's cat, was napping on the chair. She gently picked him up, settled into the chair and lowered him onto her lap. Puddles opened one eye, purred contentedly and then promptly fell back asleep.

Gloria checked her emails, replied to messages from her two sons, who would be coming for a visit next month and then opened a new screen. Lucy had mentioned the name of Bill's sporting goods store. *All Weather, All Purpose...*

Gloria reached for her cell phone that was on the desk next to the computer. She dialed Lucy's home phone.

"Hello?"

"Hi Lucy. Gloria here. What was the name of Bill's sporting goods store? It was All something…"

"Seasons." Lucy lowered her voice. "I can't talk right now. The police are here."

Chapter 3

Gloria tightened her grip on the phone. "Call me when they're gone." She disconnected the line and set the phone down. She wondered if they would be on her doorstep next.

Her fingers flew over the keyboards as she typed in All Seasons Sporting Goods, Green Springs, Michigan." The image of a long gray building with large plate glass windows popped up on the screen. In the corner of the screen was a picture of Bill.

She clicked through the tabs at the top of the page. The store sold a variety of weapons, including rifles and handguns, along with duck calls and just about any other outdoors item under the sun.

The last tab she opened was the "about us." Gloria reached for her reading glasses and slipped them on. Front and center was a picture of Bill, surrounded by his employees.

None of the names meant anything to her, except for one – an employee by the name of Randy Volk. She wondered if perhaps Randy wasn't related to Bill.

Her eyes squinted as she studied his face. There were similar facial features and Gloria would bet money the two were somehow related.

Her eyes drifted to the woman standing on the other side of Bill. A little too close in Gloria's opinion.

Gloria squinted her eyes and leaned in. It almost looked as if Bill had his arm around the woman's waist.

She glanced down at the corner clock. It was getting late…too late to make a trip to All Seasons tonight.

Gloria jumped when her cell phone began to ring. She lifted the phone and stared at the screen. It was Lucy.

"Are they gone?

"Yes, but I think they'll be back…to arrest me!"

Gloria ran her fingers lightly over the computer keys. "What makes you think that?"

"Because they searched my shed and found a gun that matches the one that was used in Bill's shooting."

The blood drained from Gloria's face and she began to feel lightheaded.

"They said something about a knife had been used, too." Lucy went on. "I think they're headed to your place next. They kept asking how close..."

Gloria jumped. Someone was banging on her porch door.

She pushed the chair away from the desk and set Puddles on the floor. "I think they're here. I'll call you back." She hung up the phone and headed to the back door.

Gloria peeked out the side window and caught a glimpse of a man in uniform. She closed her eyes. "Dear Lord, please help Lucy and me!" was all she had time to say.

She calmly unlocked the deadbolt and pulled the door open.

The uniformed officer that stood in the doorway looked familiar. He was the same one she had met earlier.

He tipped his hat. "Good evening, Mrs. Rutherford. I'm sorry to bother you this late in the day, but wondered if you had a few minutes to spare. I would like to ask you some questions about the house across the street."

Gloria swung the door open and stepped to the side. "Please. Come in." She motioned him in. "Have a seat. Coffee?"

She knew she was jabbering at the jaws but she was nervous. She had never been on the receiving end of a police investigation. Well...maybe once, but that had been a huge misunderstanding.

Officer Burnett eased his tall frame into a chair near the door and removed his hat. "I just spoke with your friend, Lucy Carlson. It seems that Mr. Volk, the man whose body was found in the empty house across the street, was well-acquainted with Ms. Carlson."

Gloria nodded. "Yes. They knew each other." Gloria silently told herself to keep the answers as brief as possible so as not to incriminate Lucy or herself.

Burnett propped an elbow on the table. "Were you acquainted with Mr. Volk?"

"Yes. I met Mr. Volk some time ago."

"So you were aware that Ms. Carlson and Mr. Volk had dated?" he asked.

Gloria felt as if Fred Burnett were trying to trap her, to get her to say something to throw poor Lucy under the bus. She wondered if she should tell him that she wanted a lawyer present. Of course, that would make her appear guilty as all get out.

Gloria remembered hearing one time that if you didn't want to answer a question, to ask one of your own. "Is Lucy a suspect?"

Burnett shifted in his chair. "We are in the beginning stages of the investigation. No one has been ruled out as a suspect...including you."

Beads of perspiration formed on Gloria's brow. She met Burnett's gaze. She would not let this man intimidate her! She hadn't done anything wrong and neither had Lucy.

The tone of Burnett's voice and his obvious attempt at intimidation ruffled Gloria's feathers. She replied in a cool, even tone. "It seems to me that you're trying to insinuate that Lucy and I are somehow involved in Mr. Volk's demise and I can assure you that we had nothing to do with his death!"

She calmly walked over to the door and yanked it open. "Now! If you don't mind, I have had a very long day."

Burnett pushed the chair back and slowly rose. He stepped onto the porch and turned back. "I had hoped to end this visit on a different note but you leave me no choice."

He shifted his gaze and stared across the street in the direction of the farm across the road, although it was pitch black. "I intend to solve this murder case, with or without your cooperation."

Gloria's eyes narrowed. That sounded like a threat to her. She waited until Burnett reached the sidewalk before she slammed the door shut. She clicked the deadbolt in place and reached for her cell phone to call Lucy.

Lucy picked up on the first ring. "He's gone."

"W-what did he say?"

Gloria repeated the questions Burnett had asked and then told her friend how she'd gotten angry and showed him the door.

Despite the gravity of the situation, Lucy giggled. "You didn't!"

"I did," Gloria said. "But I'm not sure how much that will help our case. He'll be back. Mark my words."

Lucy said what Gloria already suspected. "He thinks that we're...or at least that I'm involved."

Gloria ran her hand through her hair. "Yes, Lucy. I'm afraid he does. That's why we have to get over to Bill's store first thing tomorrow morning." *Before they arrest one of us for Bill's murder*, she silently added.

***

Gloria tossed and turned all night. Visions of Lucy locked up behind bars filled her mind. Gloria had been behind bars once before, although it was only for one night and had been a huge misunderstanding. Lucy, on the other hand, had never been arrested.

Jail was not a pleasant experience and Gloria vowed to avoid a repeat, if possible.

She crawled out of bed early the next morning, wiggled her feet into her slippers and headed for the door.

Mally, who lay curled up in her doggie bed on the other side of the dresser, let out a low moan and rolled over to face the wall.

Gloria glanced in the dining room mirror on her way to the kitchen. Tufts of gray hair stood straight up and she patted them down as she walked.

When the coffee pot began to brew, Gloria reached for the well-worn Bible she kept on the corner curio cabinet. Bill's death lay heavy on her heart, not only for the predicament that the two women were now in, but also for Bill and his family.

She turned to 2 Corinthians 4:17-18 NIV:

"For our light and momentary troubles are achieving for us an eternal glory that far outweighs them all.

So we fix our eyes not on what is seen, but on what is unseen, since what is seen is temporary, but what is unseen is eternal."

Gloria closed her eyes and prayed for Bill's salvation, for her own salvation and her friends and family. She knew that she could be gone in the blink of an eye and vowed to take the time to tell her children and loved ones how much she loved them.

Gloria slid out of the chair and made her way over to the kitchen cupboard. She reached inside for a clean coffee cup and watched as Mally padded into the kitchen.

She filled her cup with piping hot coffee and then the two of them stepped outside and onto the porch.

A light frost covered the ground and wisps of mist escaped Gloria's mouth as she yawned. Her eyes drifted to the house across the street. Someone had intentionally left Bill's body in that house for the sole purpose of framing either Lucy or Gloria...or both of them. Someone who knew them well enough to know that the police would link the two together.

After Mally finished patrolling the perimeter of the farm and watering her favorite tree, the two of them headed back inside. Today was going to be a busy day and her first order of business was to visit All Seasons Sporting Goods.

Chapter 4

Gloria reached for the phone to call Lucy when she spied Andrea's truck as it pulled into the drive.

Gloria groaned. She had completely forgotten her promise to visit the puppy mill with Andrea and Alice that morning!

She quickly dialed Lucy's number. "I forgot I promised to visit the puppy mill this morning. Do you want to ride with me and then afterwards we can head over to Bill's store?"

Lucy paused. Gloria could hear her pup, Jasper, barking in the background. "I don't know…I'm not company material today."

"Neither am I," Gloria argued, "which is a perfect reason why the two of us need to get out of the house."

Lucy finally caved and agreed to hurry up and head over so that she could ride with Gloria.

Gloria met Andrea and Alice on the porch. The morning sun had popped up on the horizon and beamed brightly in her eyes. She shaded her eyes against the bright light. "Lucy is on her way."

While the trio waited for Lucy, Gloria explained how the police had questioned Lucy and her the night before.

Andrea frowned. "They think that you have something to do with Bill's murder?"

Gloria shrugged. She didn't have time to answer as she watched Lucy pulled into the drive and parked off to the side.

She could tell by the way that Lucy trudged across the drive that her friend was down in the dumps.

Lucy lowered her sunglasses as she headed to the steps. Gloria had a hunch that Lucy had been crying and her heart sank.

She stepped off the porch and met Lucy on the sidewalk. "I explained to Andrea and Alice that we would follow them to the Acosta's farm."

Lucy nodded.

Andrea stepped close. "I'm sorry Lucy. If there's anything I can do to help…" her voice trailed off.

"I-It's okay."

It was bad enough that someone Lucy had at one time cared deeply for had been murdered but it was even worse to be questioned by the police as a possible suspect!

Gloria vowed to get to the bottom of it. She glanced down at her watch. "It's time to get this show on the road."

With a purposeful stride, she made her way over to the garage and lifted the garage door. Lucy trailed behind and climbed into the passenger seat while Gloria started the car.

The ride to the Acosta farm was silent. Gloria wasn't even sure where to start to try to help her friend with the sudden turn of events.

Andrea and Alice were already on the porch talking to Mr. Acosta when Gloria pulled her car into the rutted drive.

"We talk inside." He motioned the women inside the house and over to the kitchen table.

Two young children hovered in the doorway. "These are my children, Robert and Emeline. I have a teenage daughter, too, but she is with her mother." The children smiled shyly and then darted into the other room.

"They are beautiful children," Gloria told him. "Is your wife here?" She looked around.

"No. My wife, Maria, she moved back to New York. She did not want to live in the country," Marco Acosta explained.

Open mouth. Insert foot! Gloria had a sudden urge to have the floor open up and swallow her. "I am so sorry."

She quickly changed the subject. "I'm sure that helping others will make this all worthwhile."

Gloria turned the meeting over to Alice, who had done a great deal of research on rescue dogs and their training.

Gloria listened with interest and almost, not quite, but almost forgot about the dark cloud looming over her head...namely Bill's recent demise.

Alice explained that start-up costs for the training center would be high unless they combined it with a dog sitting service. "We need a website," she told them.

Gloria raised both hands. "Not me. My internet skills are basic at best."

The group turned expectant eyes to Andrea, the youngest person sitting at the table. She shook her head. "I'm sorry folks, but I am no expert." She had a sudden thought. "But Brian is handy at creating websites."

Gloria lifted a brow. It was true. Brian owned several small businesses in the Town of Belhaven. Maybe they could recruit him.

Alice pulled several sheets of paper from a manila folder she had brought with her. "We visited a few of the local animal kennels and a larger training facility in Grand Rapids."

She outlined the general plan and Gloria was impressed with Alice's knowledge of kennels and the research she had done.

With a plan in place and Gloria's commitment to help with the first six months of expenses, the meeting ended.

Gloria got a good feel for Marco Acosta. She felt bad about his wife, Maria, leaving him.

Before they left, Gloria and the girls stopped out back to check on the pups. The conditions were as deplorable as Gloria remembered and Alice vowed to come back first thing in the morning to start working on the living conditions.

Gloria scribbled out a check for the first month's expenses, handed the check to Alice and then climbed into the car.

Lucy climbed in next to her. She reached for her seatbelt. "You have the most generous heart out of anyone I know," Lucy told her.

"I-..." Gloria was about to disagree but quickly changed her mind. She did try.

Gloria was no saint and could be just as selfish and judgmental as the next person could. Still, it was nice to be on the receiving end of a compliment. "Thanks, Lucy," she simply said.

The girls stayed on the safe subject of the puppy project they had dubbed, "At Your Service Dogs," with

Lucy volunteering a few hours each week to help the girls get the business up and running.

Lucy directed Gloria to Four Seasons Sporting Goods in Green Springs. The first thing Gloria noticed when she pulled in the parking lot was that it was empty. "Is this place even open?" She shifted the car in park and turned the engine off.

Lucy grabbed the door handle. "Maybe they closed shop."

The women slid out of the car and wandered to the front door. The lights were on and when they pushed on the door, it swung open.

Gloria followed Lucy down the center aisle to the counter located in the back of the store. She glanced from side to side as she noted the wide variety of outdoor enthusiast items.

Behind the counter stood a man that Gloria recognized from the photo she had seen online. He was the man that resembled Bill.

Standing next to him was a younger man she guessed to be in his early twenties. The last person behind the counter was a woman. Gloria recognized her as the woman in the picture that appeared to cozy up to Bill.

When they got close, Gloria could read the man's nametag: *Randy*. She hung back and let Lucy take the lead.

Randy eyed the women with interest. His gaze turned to Lucy. "Hello Lucy."

Lucy tucked a stray strand of red hair behind her ear. "Hello Randy. I...we...stopped by to offer our condolences."

Randy's gaze turned to Gloria. "Thank you. We're still in shock."

Lucy nodded. "I'm sure. I still can't believe Bill is gone..." her voice trailed off.

"Police were by here earlier asking questions about Bill. They told us his body had been found in a vacant farmhouse not far from your place." Gloria could've sworn she noted a flicker of accusation cross his face.

Gloria didn't dare mention that the place he'd been found was directly across the street from her. "You're Bill's brother. Who do you think had it in for him?"

Randy shrugged. "I have no idea."

The dark-haired woman standing next to Randy suddenly spoke. "The only person I can think of would be Lucy," she blurted out.

Lucy began to shake her head. "No..."

Gloria lowered her gaze to read the woman's tag. *Barbara* stepped closer. The woman crossed her arms and shifted her stance. "Bill said that there was some bad blood between you and that you refused to return some of the guns he had loaned you."

Lucy rubbed the palm of her hand on the top of her jeans. "No! That's not true. I never borrowed anything from Bill. I own every single gun that I have and I can prove it." Lucy's face turned as red as her hair.

Barbara's eyes sparked. "I think that is a bald-faced lie and I told the police that they should take a close look at you."

"Why, I!" Lucy pointed at the woman's nametag. "Hey! I know who you are! Bill told me months ago, before we broke up that you were chasing after him!"

She handed her purse to Gloria. "You're one of the reasons we broke up!"

Gloria could tell by the wild look in Lucy's eyes that things were about to head south...to the Mexican border south. She slung both purses over her shoulder and reached for Lucy's arm. "Maybe we should go."

It was as if Lucy hadn't even heard Gloria. Her full attention focused on the woman on the other side of the counter.

"Why don't we step outside," Lucy challenged.

The woman – Barbara – rolled up her sleeves. "Why don't we?"

Visions of Lucy and this Barbara woman rolling around on the ground, punching each other and pulling each other's hair flashed across Gloria's mind.

Apparently, Randy had the same thought and he reached for Barbara's arm. "It's not worth it, Barb," he reasoned.

The young man behind the counter mysteriously disappeared in the midst of the conflict...w*hat if was calling the cops?*

"Let's go, Lucy," Gloria urged. She tugged on Lucy's arm.

The women retraced their steps and exited the store. Gloria kept a firm grip on Lucy's arm as she led her to the car.

"Psst!"

Gloria shifted her attention as she gazed over the roof of the car.

"Over here!" The young man who had been behind the counter, was motioning for Gloria to come over.

Gloria glanced inside the store and then casually made her way around the front of the car.

Lucy started to follow Gloria but Gloria waved her back to the car. She didn't want to draw attention…at least no more attention than they already had!

The young man, Zeke, according to the name embroidered on his shirt, motioned her forward. "Something funny was goin' on here right before Mr. Volk's death," he said. "Mr. Volk asked me to keep an eye on the cash register. He thought one of the other workers was stealing from him."

Gloria leaned in. "Did you tell the police that?"

Zeke plucked a pack of cigarettes from his front pocket. He tapped the pack on the side of his hand and pulled one out. "Nope. The police questioned us at the same time and I didn't want to say anything in front of the others."

Gloria nodded. Smart move. Otherwise, it might put a target on his back. "You need to talk to Officer Fred Burnett," she said.

Zeke clamped the cigarette between his lips and fumbled in his pants pocket for his lighter. "Yes, ma'am. I'm going to do that just as soon as I leave work today."

Gloria heard a car door slam in the distance. "Who do you think killed Mr. Volk?" she asked.

Zeke lit the cigarette and took a drag. "Could be one of the people that worked at the store. There was also a weirdo gun salesman that kept coming in. Every time he showed up, Mr. Volk would disappear in the back of the store and tell us to tell him that he wasn't here."

"Did you get a name?" This could be a huge clue!

"Maxim. Something Maxim." Zeke flicked a cigarette ash on the sidewalk. "All I know is he avoided this Maxim guy like the plague."

"Zeke!" Someone from behind the store called Zeke's name.

"Look. I gotta go!" Zeke dropped the cigarette on the cement and crushed it with the tip of his shoe. He jogged down the sidewalk that ran next to the building and disappeared from sight.

Gloria slowly walked back to the car. She opened the driver's side door and slid into the seat. "Did Bill ever mention someone by the name of Maxim?"

Lucy frowned. "Hmm. Maybe."

Gloria fastened her seatbelt and started the car.

"I think I remember..." Lucy rubbed her forehead. "Yeah! Bill hated the guy. He was some sort of salesman, always trying to pressure Bill into buying more guns and ammo."

Lucy gazed out the window as Gloria pulled onto the road. "He sold a special kind of gun. It was real expensive."

Lucy turned to face Gloria. "Oh my gosh, Gloria! The gun. The special gun. It was a Kahr® brand. It's the same gun that I have and the same one that the police told me killed Bill!"

Chapter 5

Gloria's head was spinning. First, there were the employees at All Seasons Sporting Goods who may or may not have been stealing. The woman, Barbara, who all but accused Lucy of killing Bill, and now this "Maxim" guy who Bill did not care for and sold Bill the custom gun that had, in fact, killed him. She added all of them to her mental list of suspects and included the employee, Zeke.

He seemed eager to throw others under the bus, but he was an employee, too. Maybe he was under suspicion for stealing, as well. He said that Bill told him to keep an eye on the others, but why would Bill have ruled him out as a possible thief?

Lucy and Gloria discussed the list of suspects on their way home. The next step in the investigation was to get inside the house across the street to see if there were any clues investigators may have missed.

Lucy read Gloria's mind. "We need to sneak into that house. The sooner the better."

When they reached the Town of Belhaven, Gloria made a last minute decision to stop by Dot's Restaurant.

Dot spotted the girls when they stepped through the door. She met them at a back table with a cup of coffee for Gloria and a cup of hot water, along with a packet of hot chocolate for Lucy.

Gloria caught a whiff of chicken and dumplings. Dot's famous chicken and dumplings to be exact. Her stomach grumbled. "I'm starving." She had been in such a hurry to start the investigation she had skipped breakfast.

"Me too," Lucy said. "I'll take the chicken and dumplings."

"Ditto," Gloria agreed.

Dot pulled her order pad from her apron pocket and jotted their orders down. "How is the investigation going?"

Gloria lifted the coffee cup to her lips and sipped. "We're racking up more suspects than Carter has liver pills."

Dot snorted. "So I guess the case is in high gear."

Lucy dumped the packet of hot chocolate in her cup. She added hot water, three packets of sugar and picked up her spoon. "We're hoping to lock onto something before one of us ends up in jail, charged with Bill's murder."

Dot set the coffee pot on the edge of the table. "Are you serious? You two are suspects?"

At one time or another, each of the Garden Girls had been the subject of a criminal investigation. Everyone that is, except for Lucy and Gloria. And maybe Margaret.

Lucy lifted her mug of hot chocolate and sipped. "Needs a little more sugar." She reached for another sugar packet.

Gloria explained how the gun that had killed Bill was a custom gun, one that he carried in his shop and the same brand gun that Lucy owned.

Gloria told Dot about Officer Burnett's visit the evening before and how she had politely shown him the door. "I think I've managed to make it to the suspect list."

"Maybe the detective thinks that you're covering for Lucy," Dot pointed out.

"Or that I'm an accomplice," Gloria added. "That's why Lucy and I are going to sneak into the house across the street later tonight to search for clues."

She knew they were grasping at straws. The investigators had been across the street several times and she was certain they had probably turned up anything and everything that looked suspicious. Still, they had to try...

Dot picked up the coffee pot and turned to go. "I'm not sure that's a good idea. The last thing you need is to get caught inside that house!"

In the back of Gloria's mind, the warning bells went off. Dot was right. It wouldn't look good.

Looking back, she wished she had heeded Dot's warning and her own feeling of foreboding.

***

The girls stepped out onto the back porch and Gloria stared up at the sky. It was pitch black. A thick layer of clouds hung in the air, obliterating the stars and moon.

Gloria took the lead as she and Lucy crept across the deserted street. She reached a hand inside her jacket pocket and touched the top of her 9mm handgun, safely tucked inside.

Gloria couldn't shake the feeling that the outcome of this covert operation was going to end badly.

At best, they ran the risk of getting caught and being charged with breaking and entering...but only if the new owners decided to press charges...she hoped not.

At worst, the killer could return to the scene of the crime and add two more notches to his belt: the two of them.

Gloria pushed aside the nagging thought of something going awry. After all, who in their right mind would show up this late at night?

The girls had decided not to share their plan with anyone and Dot swore she wouldn't breathe a word.

Gloria had even had to tell Paul that she would have to call him a little later than normal because something unexpected had come up.

He seemed curious but didn't press. He knew his betrothed well enough to know that she was more than likely up to something and that he more than likely did not want to know what that something was.

"You got it?" Gloria whispered to Lucy, who crept silently next to her.

Lucy nodded. "Yep." She lifted the mini flashlight and held it out.

A loud thumping echoed in the still night air. It sounded like it was coming from the old corncrib behind the barn.

Lucy tugged on Gloria's coat sleeve. "What was that?"

"I-I don't know," Gloria answered. The hair on the back of her neck stood straight out. Something felt wrong...terribly wrong. She prayed they weren't walking into a trap, that the killer hadn't returned for some unfinished business, namely them!

Gloria swallowed the lump in her throat and pushed back the feeling of dread. "Let's get this over with."

The girls tiptoed across the gravel drive and around to the back door. Gloria reached for the handle. The door was locked.

"It's locked," Gloria hissed.

Lucy reached inside her back pocket. "That's okay. I think I can open it."

Gloria stepped to the side and Lucy stepped in front of the door. She shoved what appeared to be a credit card, in between the door and the jamb. She slowly slid the card down as she turned the knob.

"Pop!" The door creaked open.

Gloria shook her head. "The Jill of all Trades," she joked.

Gloria reached inside her other pocket and pulled out a small flashlight. She turned it on and pointed the beam at the floor. "Where did you learn that trick? Never mind. Maybe I don't want to know."

She took a step inside the kitchen. The floorboards creaked under the weight.

"Shh!" Lucy whispered.

"I can't shh," Gloria said.

"Then let's hurry up," Lucy urged. "What's the plan?"

Gloria didn't have a plan. It had been years since Gloria had been inside the old farmhouse. She vaguely remembered that the kitchen was located in the back.

"Time is of the essence." Lucy reached for her own flashlight and flipped the switch. "You start over there and I'll start here."

The girls methodically searched the small kitchen…or what was left of it. The house was in the midst of major renovations. A few of the lower cabinets were still there but all of the upper cabinets were missing.

Gloria made a mental note to try to find out the names of the construction workers on site. What if one of them had taken Bill out? It was a stretch but they certainly had access to the house…

"There's nothing here." Lucy turned to Gloria. "I wish we knew where Bill's…uh, where Bill had been found."

"Let's try the other room," Gloria suggested. She pointed her flashlight at the floor and crept forward.

Lucy was right on Gloria's heel as the women made their way into the living room.

Gloria beamed the light around the room. Furniture crowded the center. Large sheets of cloth covered each of the pieces. She guessed this was to keep them from getting dirty during construction.

Gloria lifted the corner of a sheet and peeked underneath. It was a chair and it looked vaguely familiar. She wondered if it was something James' brother had left behind.

Lucy stuck close to Gloria as she studied the small room. "This place is giving me the heebie-jeebies!"

It was giving Gloria the willies, too. Just the fact that a murderer had been inside the house was enough to cause her stomach to twist in knots.

"Let's search the bedrooms," Gloria suggested. She led the way as the women quietly stepped into the first bedroom. Her eyes had adjusted to the lack of light and she pointed her flashlight at the floor.

The room was empty. Off to the far right was a closet, the door closed.

Gloria eyed the door cautiously. Did she really want to look inside?

Gloria pushed her fear aside. This was the whole reason they were there. She stiffened her back. "Let's finish this."

Before she could change her mind, she grabbed the handle of the door and yanked it open. Something large and black shot out at Gloria. She stumbled backwards. "Agh!"

Lucy, certain that Gloria was under attack, bolted from the room.

The dark object whacked Gloria on the forehead. She clenched both fists and swung at it furiously. She wasn't going down without a fight!

When it didn't fight back, she opened her eyes. It was the handle of a broom!

Gloria shoved the broom back inside the closet. "It was just a broom," she hollered into the living room.

"Scaredy cat," she mumbled under her breath.

Lucy scurried back inside the bedroom. "I was going for help!"

"Sure you were," Gloria laughed. "I could've been dead by now."

The girls finished their search of both bedrooms and a small bath located between the two bedrooms.

Gloria flicked the flashlight off. "It's hard to tell if there's a clue or not. I'm gonna go with the place is clean."

"Yeah. Let's get out of here," Lucy agreed.

The girls turned back toward the kitchen when a noise on the front porch caused them to stop dead in their tracks.

"Did you hear that?" Gloria whispered.

"Uh-huh. W-what was it?" Lucy asked.

Gloria slowly turned her gaze to the front door. She could see the shadow of someone through the glass pane. "There's someone at the door."

Just then, the doorknob began to rattle. Whoever was at the door was trying to get in!

Chapter 6

"Hit the deck!" Gloria grabbed Lucy's hand and dragged her down. The girls landed on the floor with a dull thud.

"Follow me!" Gloria slithered along the scuffed wooden floor in a desperate attempt to reach the kitchen – and the back door.

She cast a furtive glance behind her. The shadowy figure was still there and the knob rattled again. It echoed loudly in the quiet of the house. It sounded to Gloria like the rattle of death.

Lucy, who was right behind Gloria and gaining quickly, grabbed the heel of Gloria's sneaker. "Get your gun out!"

Gloria had almost forgotten she'd brought her handgun with her! She twisted to the side, fumbled inside the pocket of her jacket and reached for her gun. It wasn't there. "I-It must've fallen out of my pocket when I hit the floor," she gasped.

Lucy spun like a kid on a merry-go-round and headed back to where they'd made contact with the floor. The palms of her hands darted back and forth as she searched in vain for the cool metal of the weapon.

Gloria turned back, too, frantically sweeping her arm across the floor as she searched for the missing weapon.

Gloria glanced up at the door. The shadow was gone, along with whoever had been trying to get in!

She knew it was too good to be true. "You don't think..."

A beam of bright light shone in through the back door and illuminated a section of the living room floor. The girls froze. Gloria squeezed her eyes shut and offered up a silent prayer for protection.

***

"Hello?" The voice...male, was very familiar. "Gloria? Are you in here?"

Gloria's eyes shot open. "Paul?"

"Where are you?" The beam of light illuminated the living room and bounced off the wall. Finally, it came to rest on two sets of terrified eyes.

Gloria felt a wave of relief flood her body and sudden tears burned the back of her eyes.

The girls slowly rose to their feet.

"What are you doing here?" Gloria brushed at the sleeves of her shirt.

Lucy raised a hand in greeting. "Hi Paul."

"Hello Lucy," he answered and then turned to Gloria.

"What am I doing here?" Paul asked. "What are *you* two doing here?"

"We...uh..."

Paul shook his head. "I know what you're doing. Do you have any idea how much trouble you two could get into?"

Gloria had an inkling. But they were already in trouble so heaping a little more on top seemed insignificant, although she didn't tell Paul that.

"How did you find us?" Gloria brushed the dust bunnies from the front of her pants; her eyes casually scanned the floor in search of her gun, which was still MIA.

He nodded across the road. "I had a sneaky suspicion you were up to something so I thought I'd drop by. When I saw Mally wandering around the yard, Lucy's jeep in the drive and neither of you in sight, I put two and two together."

Lucy slid her foot across the smooth floor and made contact with the gun. She casually reached down and picked it up. "You sure got Gloria pegged," she joked.

Gloria shot her a death look as Lucy tried to slip the gun in the waistband of her pants.

Paul's sharp eye didn't miss a thing. "You brought your gun with you?"

"Well..."

"Not only did you bring your gun with you, you lost it? What if I had been the killer, found your gun and then shot you with your own weapon?"

This was as close Paul had ever come to scolding her errant behavior. Gloria looked properly contrite. "I'm sorry."

Paul, feeling bad for the tone he had just used and knowing that Gloria's heart was in the right place, wrapped an arm around her and pulled her close. "You're going to give me more gray hairs than I already have," he complained.

Gloria snuggled against Paul for a moment and then pulled back. "I think we're running out of time. My gut tells me that Officer Burnett is waiting to pounce," she predicted.

The trio wandered out the back door. Paul reached behind him, pulled the door shut and wiggled the knob to make sure it had locked. "How did you get in?"

Lucy pulled her local grocery store rewards card from her pocket. "I used this."

Paul led the way across the drive and to the edge of the road. "Lucy Carlson, I do believe you have missed your calling."

Lucy grinned. "Me too." Her smile vanished and she turned to her best friend. "I'm sorry to drag you into all of this," she apologized.

Gloria patted her arm. "You know that's not true. I was more than willing to jump into this investigation with both feet. On top of that, I'm sure I'm on the suspect list too," she pointed out.

Back inside the house, Gloria started a fresh pot of coffee while she explained to Paul what the All Seasons Sporting Goods employee, Zeke, had told her.

Paul poured a small amount of milk into his coffee cup and stirred. "Sounds to me like this Zeke character is throwing everyone under the bus but himself."

Gloria thought the same thing. There was no way to corroborate his story, especially the part about Bill telling him to keep an eye on the other employees.

Gloria dropped into the chair next to Paul and turned to Lucy. "That woman...Barbara. What's her story?"

Lucy explained that she had started working at Bill's store a few months before the two of them broke up. She said that Bill had told her the woman flirted with him all the time and that he had started to avoid her.

He had been trying to figure out how to let her go without bringing an unlawful termination of employment suit against him…or worse yet, sexual harassment.

Lucy turned the coffee cup in small circles. "Next thing I know, we break up and the two of them are dating."

"What about Bill's brother, Randy? Any bad blood there?" Gloria probed.

Lucy shrugged her shoulders. "He never said anything negative about Randy but I sometimes got the feeling that the two of them didn't get along."

Gloria tapped the tabletop with her fingernails. "So far we've got Zeke, Randy, the brother, Barbara, the on-again-off-again girlfriend and this Maxim guy that Bill didn't like."

Paul slid his chair back and stood. "I need to get back to the station." He pulled Gloria close and kissed her soundly on the lips.

Lucy covered her eyes and lowered her head. "Get a room," she teased.

Gloria giggled. "Won't be long now 'til wedding bells ring." She frowned. "Unless I'm too much to handle."

"No way," Paul said as he reached for the doorknob. "I kinda like you keeping me on my toes." He sighed as he pulled the door open. "Although it would be nice if maybe you took up something safe, like crocheting or pottery…"

Lucy snorted. "Pottery? I'd like to see that!"

Gloria walked Paul out to his patrol car. He slid into the driver's seat, pulled the door shut and rolled down the window. He cast an uneasy glance in the mirror at the dark house across the street. "Call it a cop's intuition or just worrying about the love of my life, I have an uneasy feeling about this."

Gloria did, too, and Paul just confirmed her own thoughts. She leaned her head inside the window, closed her eyes and savored the sweet, tender kiss. When she pulled away, she lifted her hands above her head and stretched her back.

"Dinner tomorrow?" She had promised to make him a home-cooked meal. It would be nice to have quiet evening at home.

Paul nodded. "Can't wait. I've been looking forward to it all week." He blew Gloria a kiss, backed the patrol car out of the drive and waved as he drove off.

Lucy met her on the sidewalk, purse in hand. "I should get going. Jasper doesn't like to be left home alone after dark."

Lucy climbed into the jeep and slid the key into the ignition. She cast a wary glance back. "Better lock the doors as soon as you get inside," she warned.

Gloria nodded. "I will. Talk to you in the morning." She watched until Lucy's taillights disappeared from sight before she slowly shuffled back into the house.

***

Gloria dreamt that her grandsons, Tyler and Ryan, were visiting. They had decided to remodel the tree fort out front.

She was in the backyard hanging clothes on the line. She clipped the last clothespin to the edge of her blouse and picked up the laundry basket. Mally ran ahead and Gloria brought up the rear.

Gloria followed the sound of the hammering but when she got to the front yard, it was empty. The boys weren't in the treehouse but the pounding continued.

Through the haze of the dream, Gloria realized that the noise was real and it wasn't her grandsons at all. Someone was tapping on her bedroom window.

Gloria bolted upright in bed. She swung her feet over the edge of the bed and scooted to the window. She lifted the edge of the blind and peeked out.

Margaret was on the other side. She motioned frantically for Gloria to let her in.

Gloria cupped her hands to her mouth. "Go around."

Margaret disappeared and Gloria headed for the door. She grabbed her robe as she passed by the bed and glanced at the clock. It was 7:15 in the morning!

Gloria's heart began to race as she picked up the pace. Something was terribly wrong for Margaret to be pounding on her bedroom window at the crack of dawn!

Mally was already waiting at the door.

Gloria opened the door to let Margaret in and Mally out.

Margaret reached out and patted Mally's fur as the dog made a beeline for her favorite watering tree.

"Is everything okay?" Gloria asked as she swung the door open.

"No!" Margaret said. "The police picked Lucy up first thing this morning. Ruth just told me they took her to jail!"

Chapter 7

Gloria's mouth dropped open and she stared at Margaret, speechless. She had feared this moment was coming and had prayed before she went to bed the night before that it wasn't but that nagging feeling that something bad was about to happen hung in the back of her mind.

"What…"

"Ruth was on her way to work and saw the cops putting Lucy in the back of the cop car," Margaret blurted out. "When I stopped by the post office to drop some stuff in the box out front, Ruth met me at the door. She said Officer Nelson had just been by and he told her they picked Lucy up. He said they were going to charge her with Bill's murder!"

The blood drained from Gloria's face. Poor Lucy! She had never been booked before, unlike Gloria, Margaret and Gloria's sister, Liz. It was an unpleasant experience and one that Gloria hoped she would never have to go through again.

Gloria motioned her into the kitchen and slowly walked over to the coffee pot. She poured the leftover coffee from the night before into clean cups and put both cups in the microwave. Normally, Gloria would have brewed a fresh pot but her mind was numb.

Margaret pulled out a kitchen chair and plopped down. "What are we going to do?"

"Call Paul." Gloria reached for her phone. The call went right to voice mail and Gloria had a hunch he was sleeping since he had worked the night before. "I'll have to wait. Maybe we should run down to the station. I can post bond."

"We need a lawyer," Margaret said.

"Right." Gloria nodded. "Brian should be able to point us in the right direction."

Just then, Dot's van pulled in behind Margaret's SUV. News sure did travel fast in the small Town of Belhaven. "You talk to Dot while I go get ready."

Gloria disappeared into the dining room and raced to the bedroom to grab some clean clothes. Her mind spun recklessly. What kind of evidence could the police possibly have to arrest Lucy?

Gloria emerged from the bathroom a short time later. Not only was Dot and Margaret there, Andrea and Ruth had arrived and the group of Garden Girls, minus Lucy, gathered around the kitchen table.

The girls looked at Gloria expectantly.

Dot spoke first. "This is a 911 Garden Girls emergency. What do we do?"

"Coffee. We need coffee to clear the cobwebs." Gloria made a beeline for the coffee pot. She filled the pot with water, popped a new filter into the basket, poured fresh coffee grounds inside the basket and then filled the reservoir before turning it to on.

The girls slid their chairs to the side to make room for Gloria. "The first thing we need to do is pray."

The girls promptly reached for each other's hand and bowed their heads. "Dear Lord. You know that our friend, Lucy, is in jail this morning, charged with a crime she didn't commit. Lord, we ask You to help us solve the murder and track down the true killer." Gloria didn't know what else to add so she ended it with, "Amen."

Dot uncovered a box of tasty looking pastries and donuts as Gloria set a cup in front of each of her friends. She poured freshly brewed coffee into each cup.

All of them eyed the tempting treats with the same thought in mind. Lucy was the sweet tooth of the bunch and just the sight of the goodies made Gloria's stomach churn.

"I don't think I can eat these," she admitted.

Andrea shook her head. "Me either."

They unanimously agreed that the sight of Lucy's favorite food caused them to lose their appetites.

Dot replaced the lid on the treats and pushed them off to the side. "What do we do?"

"The first thing we need to do is see if we can get Lucy out of jail," Gloria said.

She went on. "Then, we have to get serious about solving this case." She left the words unspoken that it was either that, or chance one of their closest friends being convicted of a crime she didn't commit.

Ruth lifted her cup to her lips and eyed Gloria over the rim. "What about Paul?"

"I left him a message." Gloria glanced at the clock above the sink. "Don't you have to work?" It was just after eight in the morning.

Ruth shook her head. "Kenny is holding down the fort." Kenny was Ruth's right hand man at the post office. When he found out one of the girls was in trouble, he offered to cover for Ruth until she could make it in.

Andrea nodded. "Maybe I should call Brian to see if he can recommend an attorney."

"Great minds think alike," Gloria said. "Margaret said the same thing."

Andrea reached for her cell phone while Gloria poured the last of the coffee and headed to the kitchen counter to brew another pot. While the coffee was brewing, she told the girls what had happened so far and ticked off the list of suspects.

Margaret wiped an imaginary crumb off the table. "Someone needs to do a little snooping around Four Seasons Sporting Goods."

Ruth raised a brow. "Maybe look into ordering one of those guns. Like the one that killed Bill," she suggested.

Gloria wandered over to the counter and reached for the pot of coffee. "I'd love to but Lucy and I were in there yesterday. They would recognize me."

"True." Andrea dropped her chin on top of her fist. "I know enough about guns. Not as much as Lucy, for sure. But I'll go if one of you will go with me."

Ruth shook her head. "I'd go but I have to work."

"I can go in a pinch," Dot offered.

Margaret held up a hand. "The most obvious choice would be me. I can go. Besides, Don and I have been talking about buying a gun for protection, what with the way the world is today."

All heads turned to Margaret.

"You don't have a gun?" Gloria was surprised. Margaret and her husband, Don, were two of the wealthier residents in their small town. Don had retired a couple years earlier as vice president of a local bank. "Why that's your second amendment right."

Margaret frowned. "There was never a need."

She had a point. The Town of Belhaven was relatively crime free...except for the murder of Andrea's first husband, whose body had been discovered in the woods out back of the old elementary school. Or the time there was a large drug trafficking ring operating out of the post office. Then there was the time...

"I take that back," Margaret thought about her answer. "Yeah. It's probably time to buy a weapon."

The girls decided to divide and conquer. Andrea and Margaret would head over to All Seasons Sporting Goods to do a little investigative work.

Dot would stop by Nails and Knobs, Brian's hardware store, to see if he could recommend a good attorney.

Ruth had to head back to work so Kenny could start his route but promised she would keep her ear to the ground.

Gloria would be the one to drive to the police station to see if she could spring Lucy.

The girls agreed to meet at Dot's Restaurant around five and each of them headed out.

Dot was the last to leave. She reached for her purse and then paused. "I know you love Lucy with all your heart. You love all of us, and that you're worried sick. Just be careful, Gloria. Sometimes I think you carry the weight of the world on your shoulders."

Dot impulsively reached over and hugged her friend's neck. A lone tear trickled down Gloria's cheek as she watched Dot make her way back to her van. The stress of the last couple of days was wearing on her and at that moment, she felt every single one of her sixty some years.

Gloria slowly closed the door, leaned her head against the glass pane and let the tears flow. When she lifted her head, she wiped the wetness from her cheeks and stiffened her back. Lucy needed her and Gloria was not going to let her down!

Gloria grabbed her purse from the chair, her car keys from the hook near the door and stepped out onto the porch. It was time to bring Lucy home!

***

The Kensington County Sheriff's station was abuzz with activity. Gloria had to circle the parking lot twice before she was able to squeeze Annabelle into a spot near the back.

She shut the engine off and reached for the door handle before she paused to bow her head and pray a quick prayer that they would allow her to post Lucy's bail and take her home.

It was 11:45 in the morning, which meant that, according to Ruth, the police had picked Lucy up over four hours ago.

Gloria hoped that the interrogations had ended and Lucy had been booked. She frowned as she wondered if bail had even been set. If not, this trip would be a waste of time.

Gloria stepped inside the cold, drab lobby and approached the counter. A dark-haired woman in a police uniform looked up from her computer. "Yes, can I help you?"

Gloria nodded. "I'm looking for my friend, Lucy Carlson." She didn't know what else to say so she closed her mouth and waited.

She lowered her gaze and read the woman's tag. Her name was Lisa. "Let me check to see if we have anyone here by that name." The woman turned her attention to the computer screen in front of her and began to tap on the keyboard.

She frowned and then looked back up. "You said Ms. Carlson was a friend of yours?"

Gloria nodded. "I-I'm not certain if she's been arrested or was picked up for questioning..." her voice trailed off. She wasn't sure on the police lingo.

Although Gloria's favorite TV show was *Detective on the Side* and she hardly missed an episode, she wasn't sure if she had explained it right.

The woman, Lisa, nodded. "Yes. She's here."

Gloria set her purse on the counter. "Can I see her?"

The woman held up an index finger. "I'll check."

Lisa stepped over to a door on the far side of the lobby area and disappeared behind it.

Gloria wandered over to the "Wanted Posters." Her mind must have been playing tricks on her because several of the people in the mugshots looked familiar, although she wasn't sure why.

She shrugged her shoulders, certain that she was under extreme duress and the people in the pictures could not possibly be anyone she knew.

"Yes, ma'am."

Gloria spun around. Lisa had returned.

"Ms. Carlson is free to leave. She's in the waiting room across the hall."

Lisa pointed to a door on the right.

Gloria smiled. "Thank you...Lisa."

The woman returned the smile and switched her attention back to the computer screen.

Gloria crossed the room, grabbed the door handle and pulled it open. On the other side of the door was a small hall and across the hall was another door.

She stepped inside the room and gazed around. Her heart sank when she caught a glimpse of Lucy's bright red head bent down, her hands covering her face.

Gloria tiptoed over to the corner chair. She eased down in the chair next to Lucy. "Hey, Lucy."

Lucy's head popped up. Her eyes, red and bloodshot, met Gloria's eyes.

Gloria reached out and grabbed her friend's hand. "I'm here to take you home," she simply said.

The two women rose to their feet and silently walked out of the Kensington County Sheriff's station.

Chapter 8

Lucy stared out the window the entire ride home. Gloria, determined to give her friend the space she needed, focused on the road ahead.

When they reached the outer edges of Belhaven, Lucy spoke. "Can we stop by the cemetery?"

"Sure." Gloria nodded. Gary, Lucy's first husband, was buried in the cemetery.

Gloria's husband, James, was buried in the same cemetery, but his grave was in a different section.

Gloria pulled Annabelle into the cemetery grounds and eased down the narrow dirt path. She stopped the car adjacent to Gary's headstone.

She shifted the car into park and watched as Lucy climbed out of the passenger seat.

The wind had picked up. Lucy pulled her jacket tightly around her thin frame and lowered her head.

Gloria's heart broke as she watched the frail, broken figure shuffle to the gravesite.

Lucy dropped to her knees. She rubbed a light hand across the letters, *Gary Carlson*. Lucy took a deep breath and spoke to the man who had been the love of her life for decades. She poured out her heart and explained her situation.

When she finished, Lucy wiped the tears on her face with the back of her jacket. She placed both hands on the cold, hard ground and pushed herself to a standing position. She stood, looking down at the grave one final time before she turned on her heel and made her way back to the car.

She opened the door of the car, eased into the passenger seat and reached for her seatbelt. "Thank you for waiting for me, Gloria. I feel much better now."

Lucy clicked the lock in place and turned to Gloria. "It's time to stop messing around and track down whoever it is that's trying to frame me!"

The old Lucy was back and Gloria shifted the car into drive as they headed out of the cemetery. "You betcha Lucy! That's exactly what we're going to do," Gloria vowed.

The girls swung by Lucy's place so she could let Jasper out for a run before they drove to the farm.

Gloria parked in front of the garage and the girls headed inside the house where they hung their jackets on hooks just inside the door.

Lucy dropped her purse on an empty chair and eyed the box of baked goods that Dot had left behind.

Gloria slid the box toward her friend. "Help yourself." She headed to the fridge to scrounge up something for lunch.

By the time Gloria had fixed two roasted turkey and Swiss cheese sandwiches, along with bowls of piping hot chicken noodle soup, Lucy had wolfed down one Bavarian cream donut, two pumpkin spice donuts and topped it all off with a tangy lemon bar.

She reached for a napkin and dabbed at her lips. "Those were delicious!"

Gloria set the sandwich and bowl of soup in front of Lucy. "You sure you don't want to finish it off with a cup of hot chocolate?" she teased.

Lucy shrugged as she reached for her sandwich plate. "Maybe for dessert."

Gloria eased into the seat across from her and unfolded a napkin in her lap. The girls bowed their heads in prayer and Gloria thanked the Lord that Lucy was home safe and sound.

When she finished praying, she explained to Lucy all that had happened that morning and how the girls had come up with a plan.

Lucy gazed out the window. Tears began to well in her eyes. "I don't know what I would do without my friends," she whispered in a soft voice.

Gloria lifted her soupspoon. "You would do exactly what we are doing for you."

She silently hoped that Andrea and Margaret were able to glean some information from their trip to All Seasons Sporting Goods.

***

Andrea turned into All Seasons Sporting Goods parking lot and pulled into a parking spot on the end.

Margaret unbuckled her seatbelt. "What was the name of that gun again?"

"It's a 9MM Kahr®," Andrea said. "I think I have enough questions the employees won't be able to answer and they'll have to call in that gun rep...what was his name?"

Margaret reached for her purse. "Maxim something."

The girls had decided to let Andrea do the talking. Margaret knew next to nothing about guns. Andrea had a small handgun for protection. Lucy was the weapons expert of the bunch.

The store was busy and the two women wandered around while they waited for one of the employees, a woman, to approach.

If this was Barbara, Margaret has to wonder what Bill had seen in the woman. She was short...shorter than Margaret, who stood a mere 4' 8" tall. She wore wire-rimmed glasses and her long, dark hair hung limp around her shoulders.

Lucy was a thousand times prettier!

"Can I help you?" Her green eyes peered at them through the thick frames.

Andrea shifted the purse on her shoulder. "Yes, my…"

"Mother," Margaret blurted out.

Andrea slid a sideways glance at Margaret. "My mother is looking for a handgun. Something small and easy to handle. Price isn't a concern," she added.

The woman, Barbara, lifted a brow. Andrea could almost see the commission cha-ching in her head. "Follow me."

She motioned them over to a display case off to one side. Several handguns sat on the top shelf while several larger pistols were displayed on the lower level.

Barbara fished inside her pocket and pulled out a keyring. She inserted one of the keys into the lock on the back panel, turned the key and slid the door to the side.

"This would be a good choice." She pulled out a small, silver gun and handed it to Margaret who motioned for Andrea to take it.

Andrea picked up the weapon and slowly turned it over in her hand. It was a Ruger®. "I don't like the way this one handles. Anything else?" she asked as she handed the weapon back.

Barbara nodded and reached for another gun. "This one has a different grip. You may like it better but it's more expensive." She handed it to Andrea. It was the Kahr®.

Andrea ran the tip of her finger over the cool metal of the gun. The gun was lighter than the other one and the grip was comfortable. Actually, Andrea liked the gun. "Do you have any others in this model?" Andrea knew they didn't. She had done her research on line before she left the house. There were several stair step models but the one in her hand was only one of two that All Seasons stocked.

Barbara smiled. The store carried the cheapest version of the Kahr®. The others were much more expensive...and special order. "We have two but the other one...isn't here.

Barbara took the gun from Andrea and placed it back inside the case. "Artie Maxim, our Kahr® rep, comes by every Thursday."

Tomorrow was Thursday. "Perfect." Andrea turned to Margaret. "Mom, do you have time to come back tomorrow?"

Margaret shifted her purse. "I think I can squeeze it in." She turned to the clerk. "What time?"

Barbara lifted a finger. "Let me check. I'll be right back." She disappeared in the back of the store.

Andrea turned to Margaret. "Can you come back tomorrow?"

Margaret didn't have time to answer. Barbara had returned. "He'll be here in the morning; around 9-ish is when he usually shows up."

The girls told the woman they would come back the next day and then turned to go when Andrea paused. "Say. I heard that the man who owned this place was murdered." Her eyes widened innocently.

Barbara locked the gun case and shoved the keys in her pocket. "Yeah." Barbara's expression grew solemn. "It looks like his ex-girlfriend may have been involved," she stated.

"Interesting." Margaret set her purse on the counter and leaned forward.

Andrea was certain that Margaret was ready to pop the woman in the jaw. She reached over and touched her arm.

"Why do you say that?" Andrea asked.

"I know for a fact that the ex-girlfriend had recently purchased a gun identical to the one that killed Bill," she answered. "On top of that, his body was discovered in a dilapidated old farmhouse just down the road from where the ex lives."

"Maybe someone set her up," Margaret theorized.

Barbara tapped her fingers on the top of the glass. "True. Never thought about that. Course, one of those exact same guns came up missing a couple days before Bill was murdered."

She went on. "Randy, Bill's brother, told the police about the missing gun, but I guess police uncovered more evidence that pointed to the ex. What was her name...Trudy."

Barbara rubbed the palm of her hand across the glass top. "No. That wasn't it. I can see her face." She stared up at the ceiling as if Lucy's name would magically materialize. "Kinda homely woman with bright red hair."

Andrea felt the tips of her ears burn. She slid Margaret a sideways glance.

Margaret appeared to be on the verge of lunging across the counter to attack the woman. "What about his brother, Randy?"

Barbara shrugged. "Randy. He's a nice enough guy, although now that I think about it, the two of them had a knockdown, drag out argument a couple weeks back." She shook her head. "It was a pretty tense work environment."

"What were they fighting about?" Margaret asked through thinned lips as she tried to blot out the image of Barbara's eyes bulging as she squeezed the life out of her.

Barbara shrugged. "Money. Not that I know for certain, but I do believe they were arguing about money." Barbara must have decided she had said too much. She quickly changed the subject. "So you'll be back tomorrow morning? I won't be here," she added.

Andrea fumbled with the clasp of her designer bag and reached for her truck keys. "Yes and we'll be sure to let the gun rep know that you helped us today," she assured the woman.

"Thanks. I appreciate that."

The girls stepped out of the store and made their way to the edge of the parking lot where Andrea had parked the truck.

Margaret jerked her head toward the store. "What do you think?"

Andrea clicked the key fob and unlocked the doors. "That we have too many suspects with too many motives. Maybe talking to this Maxim guy tomorrow will help."

The women climbed into the truck and headed back to Belhaven. When they turned onto Main Street, Andrea spotted Gloria's car parked in front of Dot's Restaurant. "Want to stop by?"

Margaret nodded. The girls had agreed to meet up later in the day. They were early but Margaret was starving.

Andrea pulled into an open spot and shut the engine off. She reached for the driver's side door. "Don't mention..."

"That the nasty store clerk described our Lucy in a most unflattering way? It took everything I had not to punch her in the face," Margaret admitted.

Andrea giggled. "I could tell. Just remember, the woman was after Bill while he and Lucy were dating," she reminded her.

"True." Margaret climbed out of the truck and shut the passenger door. "Still. I would've loved to inflict a little pain on that woman's pig face."

Andrea, if she were honest, would have liked to, too. Nothing was worse than having to remain silent and unable to defend their friend in the face of a blatant attack!

The girls picked up the pace as they stepped inside. It was a mini reunion as the girls celebrated Lucy's release. They hugged Lucy and thanked God that she hadn't been booked but just detained for questioning.

Dot and her husband, Ray, made their way over with glasses of ice water. "The only one missing is Ruth," she said.

Gloria reached for an ice water to lighten Dot's load. "We'll be sure to fill her in."

Lucy reached for a water and turned her attention to Andrea and Margaret. "What did you find out?"

Margaret bent down and shoved her purse under her chair. "That one of the guns, the same gun that killed Bill, came up missing from the display case a couple days before his death."

Lucy's eyes widened. "Really? The Kahr® is missing?"

Andrea nodded. "Yep. And Mom and I are going back tomorrow to talk to Maxim, the dealer."

Gloria frowned. "Mom?"

Margaret chuckled. "Yeah. We told Barbara that I was Andrea's mother and that we were in the store to shop for a handgun for me."

Margaret could easily pass for Andrea's mother. They both had light colored hair and Margaret was a good 25 years Andrea's senior. "Good cover," Gloria said. "Smart thinking."

She turned to Dot, who had stopped by Brian's hardware store earlier to ask him about attorneys, just in case Lucy would need one, although she hoped not. "What did Brian say?"

"Oh! I almost forgot!" Dot reached inside the front pocket of her apron and pulled out a slip of paper. "According to Brian, this guy is the best around. He said if you need to hire him, mention Brian's name and he'll give you a discount."

Lucy took the slip of paper, briefly glanced at the information and then shoved it in her front pants pocket. "I hope not."

Dot jotted down Margaret and Andrea's lunch orders and the group waited for her to return before they turned the conversation back to the investigation.

Dot slid into an empty seat and looked at Gloria expectantly. "Now what do we do?"

Gloria frowned as she swiped at a stray strand of hair. She didn't have a plan. They had already searched the house across the street and came up empty handed.

It looked like Margaret and Andrea had a good handle on the list of suspects.

The only thing she could think of was to get inside Bill's house to search for clues. "Too bad we can't search Bill's place," she said aloud.

Lucy grasped the end of her straw and jabbed the ice cubes inside her glass of water with the tip. "We could…I still have a key to his house."

Chapter 9

Gloria gasped. "Lucy! Why didn't you mention that before?"

Lucy fidgeted in her seat. "Well, if the police knew I had a key to his house, wouldn't that make me even more of a suspect?" she pointed out.

Gloria frowned. It was true. If the police knew that Lucy had access to Bill's house, it would certainly be a piece of incriminating evidence.

Ruth wandered in and to the back of the restaurant. "Well? What happened?" She slid into the last available chair and dropped her purse on the floor next to her.

Gloria brought her up to speed and finished with the last tidbit of information – that Lucy still had a key to Bill's house.

Ray and restaurant employee, Holly, carried two trays laden with food to the table. The girls waited until the food was on thc table before picking up where they left off.

Andrea reached for an onion ring and dipped it in her ketchup. "Are there a lot of neighbors close to Bill's place?"

Lucy shook her head. "Nope. He owns some 20 acres of land and his ranch sits smack dab in the middle of the property."

That made sense. Someone like Bill who had been an avid outdoorsman his entire life probably craved the solitude and quiet of living in the middle of nowhere.

"So it would be fairly easy to...say...stop by his place and have a look around?" Ruth inquired.

Lucy nodded. "Yep. He had a couple hunting dogs that guarded the property but I'm sure that by now, someone has picked them up."

Gloria glanced around the table. "I'm a sucker for an adventure. Who wants to go with me to have a look around?"

"I'll go with you," Lucy offered.

"But..." Gloria started to argue.

Lucy lifted a hand to stop her. "It makes sense for me to go. I know the layout of the property and house. You'd be going in blindly without me," she pointed out.

Lucy was the most logical choice to go. Still, if they were caught trespassing and Lucy was with them, it would be one more nail in Lucy's coffin, so to speak. She thought back to the close call they'd had at the farm across the street the night before.

"I'll go with you," Ruth piped up. "I can bring my drone along to do a little reconnaissance beforehand. You know, make sure the coast is clear before we try to get inside the house."

Gloria narrowed her eyes. She remembered the last time Ruth had used her drone to try to help solve a mystery and it had turned into a disaster when the drone had run out of power and gone down behind enemy lines.

But that was before Gloria and Margaret had gifted Ruth a new Phantom II drone. It had longer range and a heavy-duty battery.

Ruth noted the look of concern on Gloria's face. "Don't worry. I've been practicing with the drone you guys bought me." She rubbed her hands together. "This will be my first chance to test 'er out!"

There was no way Gloria could tell her friend "no." And, it *was* one of the reasons they had bought Ruth the drone in the first place. So that she could, at some point in time, help them out if need be. She hadn't realized it would be only days later that they would put Ruth's new toy to the test.

Gloria gazed out the large picture window thoughtfully. "So when should we go?"

Ruth popped the last piece of the BLT sandwich in her mouth and dropped the napkin on her empty plate. "The drone is hard to use when it's dark so it will have to be during the day."

She went on. "Kenny can cover for me if you want to go first thing tomorrow morning."

The trio agreed to meet at Ruth's place first thing in the morning.

While Gloria, Lucy and Ruth were breaking in…err, searching Bill's place, Andrea and Margaret would head back to All Seasons Sporting Goods to try to glean information from Artie Maxim, the sales rep.

"I guess I'll hold down the fort," Dot said. "Come back tomorrow when you're done and you can be my taste testers. I've been working on a new strawberry donut."

"Cool!" Lucy rubbed her hands together. "I'll be the official taste-tester!"

Gloria glanced at her watch. "I should get going."

Gloria and Lucy climbed back in the car. She stopped at Lucy's place to drop her off before heading home.

As soon as Gloria opened the porch door, Mally darted out into the yard.

Gloria dropped her purse on the chair, just inside the door and stepped back onto the porch. "Want to go for a walk?"

Mally, who had been sniffing around the edge of the garage, bounded across the lawn and skidded to a halt in front of Gloria. "Woof!"

Gloria took the "woof" for a yes and the two of them crossed the yard as they made their way between the empty farm fields and toward the woods out back. There were still a few hours of daylight left and it had been quite some time since their last visit to their favorite quiet spot.

Forecasters had predicted a light dusting of snow for later that evening and Gloria knew her days of long, leisurely walks in the woods would end soon. Not only would the walks end, Gloria's days of living alone were almost over.

Next month, just before Christmas, Gloria and Paul planned to marry at Andrea's place. They had originally planned an intimate affair with only family and close friends, but the guest list had ballooned and they now had over 75 confirmed guests. They were still waiting on another 40 responses but Gloria had a hunch most of them would be coming as well.

She needed to get Lucy's crisis behind her so she could focus on the wedding and the much-anticipated visit from her children and their families.

With everything that had been going on, she hadn't even had time to worry about Thanksgiving. Paul and she had decided a small turkey day would be best, but the more Gloria thought about it, she wondered if maybe instead of that, all of the girls could get together, share the cooking duties and make it a more friends and family affair. She made a mental note to discuss it with Paul before mentioning it to the girls.

Ruth had one sibling, a sister who lived in Florida. She would most likely spend Thanksgiving Day alone and that was the last thing Gloria wanted.

Dot and Ray were childless and although they had each other, it would still be a quiet day.

Lucy had told Gloria that her children planned to spend Thanksgiving with their spouses' families this year. It would be just her and her boyfriend, Max.

That left Andrea. Gloria knew her young friend had no intention of flying to New York to be with her parents. Instead, she would remain in Michigan with her former housekeeper, Alice, and Andrea's boyfriend, Brian.

The more she thought about it, the more she liked the idea of a potluck-kind-of Thanksgiving. After all, her friends *were* her family!

Mally and she had reached the edge of the woods and Mally darted off to check out the creek. The water was still low but soon, the snow would pile up and the creek would fill.

Gloria settled onto "her" log nearby and watched Mally frolic in the frigid water. She shook her head and grinned as Mally chased a bunny rabbit that had been scampering back and forth, teasing Mally, if Gloria had to guess.

Her mind drifted to Lucy's dilemma. Right now, there were several suspects. Bill's brother, Randy, who had been arguing with Bill just days before his death. Barbara, the employee who had chased after Bill and eventually dated him, even though Lucy claimed Bill never cared for the woman.

Next on the list was Zeke, the young man who seemed all too eager to throw Randy, Barbara and even this unknown Artie Maxim under the bus.

Then there was the missing gun. One of the store employees, possibly even the gun dealer, had access to the gun.

The police lacked a murder weapon, not counting Lucy's gun, which was probably why Lucy was the main suspect. She actually owned a gun exactly like the one that had killed Bill.

Gloria knew that if she could figure out what happened to the missing gun, she could figure out who had murdered Bill!

She jumped to her feet. "C'mon girl. We have some more digging to do."

Gloria zigzagged through the trees as she made her way out of the forest.

The wind had picked up and cold air blew right through her jacket. She picked up the pace as she headed back to the farm. There was a piece of the puzzle missing. If only she could figure out what it was...

Back at the house, she settled in at the desk and turned her computer on. After it warmed up, she checked her email and then started a search of the list of suspects. She searched Bill Volk and Randy Volk.

She opened a second screen and pulled up the picture of Bill and his employees. She jotted Barbara Coleman's name down and last, but not least, Zeke Waren, the young employee Gloria had talked to.

She researched both of their names but came up emptyhanded.

Frustrated, she clicked out of the screens and glanced down at her watch. It was time to start dinner.

Margaret had recently shared her secret meatloaf recipe and Gloria was anxious to try it out on Paul.

Gloria assembled the ingredients for the meatloaf and mixed them all together. When she finished, she placed the loaf inside a metal baking dish and set it on top of the stove.

She had been craving her homemade cheesy hash brown casserole. The dish would be a perfect side for the meatloaf.

Gloria pulled a large glass dish from the cabinet. Next, she mixed the thawed hash browns with a can of cream of chicken soup, sour cream, shredded cheddar cheese and melted butter. After she mixed the ingredients together, she dumped the mixture into the square casserole dish and popped both the meatloaf and casserole in the oven.

Gloria untied her apron and hung it on the hook as she glanced at the clock on the way out of the kitchen. Paul would be here in an hour and a half. It would give her plenty of time to take a long, leisurely bath.

After her recent windfall, Gloria had splurged on a bathroom remodel. The remodel included double sink granite counters, a new water saver toilet and her favorite thing of all, a large, luxurious jetted tub.

She filled the tub with hot water; added jasmine scented bath oil, peeled off her clothes and then slipped into the tub.

Gloria closed her eyes and leaned her head against the pillow rest. Should she tell Paul about the girls' plan to snoop around Bill's place in the morning?

He had been upset when he caught Lucy and her inside the house across the street. She knew he would not be happy with her if she told him their plans.

Technically, they wouldn't be breaking and entering. Lucy had a key. Bill had given it to her. If he had wanted it back, he would have asked for it. On top of that, she was certain that Bill would want someone to track down his killer. Gloria knew that if it was she, she sure would!

Gloria savored her quiet bath time until Mally began to paw at the bathroom door. She lifted her head and pulled herself to an upright position. "I'm done," she grumbled.

She let the water out of the tub and reached for a clean bath towel.

Gloria slipped into her robe and tied it tight before she let Mally outside for a brief run before she headed back to the bathroom to finish primping.

Their wedding was only a few weeks away now and Gloria was starting to have minor anxiety attacks. What if he got cold feet and left her at the altar? What if she got cold feet?

She pushed the dark thoughts aside as she popped the top off the tube of lipstick and spread the pale pink cream across her lower lip. She rubbed her lips together and nodded at her reflection in the mirror. Finally, she was ready!

"Honey, I'm home."

Gloria set the tube of lipstick on the counter and grinned. It was Paul. She had given him a key to the house a while back and told him he might as well get used to letting himself in and making himself at home.

She wandered into the kitchen and watched as he hung his jacket on the hook by the door. He held a card in his hand and when she got close, he handed it to her.

Gloria took the card. "What's this?"

"For you. Just a small treat to spoil my girl." Paul pulled Gloria close and circled his arms around her waist. He lowered his head and gently kissed her lips. "So that's what a proper kiss feels like," he teased. "It's been so long, I forgot what it felt like."

"Ha!" she snorted. "If you weren't so darn busy at work all the time." She quickly changed the subject. "So what's in the card?"

"Open it," he urged.

Gloria slid her fingernail under the edge of the envelope and lifted the lid. She slipped the card out of the envelope. On the front was a portrait of a beautiful rose garden. The inside of the card spoke words of love.

Gloria blinked back the tears. Tucked inside the envelope was a gift card for a day at the spa. "Paul! What…"

"You need a break, Gloria. You deserve a day to be pampered and spoiled and I thought this would be perfect."

Gloria pulled Paul's head toward her and kissed his lips. "You are going to spoil me rotten, if it's not already too late," she warned.

"Nah!" He said. "No chance."

The timer went off and Gloria headed to the stove. She pulled the oven door open and peered inside. The cheesy hash brown casserole bubbled merrily. She pulled the dish from the oven and then lifted the pan of meatloaf.

Gloria spread a thick layer of ketchup across the top of the meatloaf and placed it back inside the oven. "Fifteen more minutes and it'll be ready."

"It smells delicious. I can't wait 'til there's no more TV dinners," he said.

"Don't be so sure about that," Gloria warned.

She poured two glasses of tea and settled in at the table. As she sat there, she thought how comfortable it felt. How good and perfect this moment was. If this was how their marriage would be, Gloria could hardly wait!

They chatted about Paul's job and Paul asked how Gloria's day had gone. She was careful to avoid bringing up the incident from the night before when he had caught Gloria and Lucy inside the house across the street.

He, however, wasn't. Paul sipped his tea and set the glass on the table. "How's it going with Lucy?"

Gloria averted her eyes and studied her sparkling engagement ring. "Oh...okay," she answered. "The police questioned Lucy at length this morning but let her go. Brian gave us the name of a good attorney," she added.

Paul rubbed the faint five o'clock shadow on his chin thoughtfully. "Do you think that will be necessary?"

Gloria explained all that she knew. The suspects, the missing gun and she even told him about the gun dealer.

"Are you going to confront this Maxim fellow?" Paul could see his spunky bride-to-be doing exactly that.

Gloria shook her head. "Nope. Andrea and Margaret are going to meet him in the morning."

Paul slid out of his chair and stepped over to the fridge to refill his glass. "What will *you* be doing?" He knew there was no way Gloria would stand on the sidelines. She would most definitely be right in the thick of things.

Gloria decided to answer his question with a question. "What should I do?"

Paul brought the pitcher to the table and filled her glass. "You're up to something." After he filled her glass, he placed the pitcher back inside the fridge and closed the door. "I probably don't want to know."

"Probably not," she agreed.

The oven timer sounded a second time and Gloria was thankful for the interruption.

Paul set the table while Gloria carried the food and set it in the center.

They bowed their heads to pray and Gloria said a special prayer for Lucy, who was at home...alone.

She sliced a large piece of meatloaf from the center and set it on Paul's plate. "I hope you like it. This is Margaret's super-secret recipe. It took me years to wear her down and she finally shared it with me."

Paul scooped a large spoonful of cheesy hash browns on the side and then set a piece of crusty bread on his napkin.

Last, but not least, he added a pile of green beans. Gloria had canned the beans a couple months ago. She had had a bountiful crop this year and her stockpile of canned goods would last both of them through the winter, until it was time to start a garden again in the spring.

The evening flew by and before Gloria knew it, dinner was over and the kitchen cleaned. They even had time to kick back and relax in the living room with a bowl of chocolate ice cream.

When the ten o'clock news started, Paul reluctantly got to his feet. "I better head out. The kids will be waiting up for me."

Gloria frowned. Paul's son, Jeff, and his daughter-in-law, Tina, had recently moved back in with him after being evicted from the apartment they had been renting. If ever there was a problem looming on the horizon for Paul and Gloria's relationship, she guessed it would be these two.

It seemed that whenever they got into a pickle, they turned to Paul to bail them out. It wasn't that Gloria didn't want to help family, but these two seemed to cause their own difficulties. Both had steady jobs and made good money. They just did not know how to manage their finances.

Gloria had suggested several times that Paul get involved and to his credit, he had tried, but nothing seemed to change.

She had a hunch that they knew good ole dad would be there no matter what and that there were no consequences for their actions. Someday Paul...and Gloria...would be gone. She wondered who would take care of them then.

Gloria bit her tongue and let it go. She walked him to his truck and waited for him to climb in and fasten his seatbelt. He rolled down the window and leaned out. "I love you. Please try to stay out of trouble tomorrow, whatever it is you have planned."

Gloria nodded. "I'll try," she answered honestly. "Sometimes it's hard." She leaned in for a long, tender kiss and blinked back the tears that burned the back of her eyes.

Paul waited for her to wander back up the sidewalk and into the house before he backed out of the drive and pulled onto the road.

Chapter 10

Gloria woke early the next morning. It was still dark out. She could hear a hoot owl off in the distance...the same owl that returned every November. She had come to expect the owl, to wait for his call.

The first time she had noticed his haunting hoot was the same year that James died. Maybe she hadn't noticed before because she never paid close attention to the noises. After James was gone, she would lie awake in bed for hours listening to every creak, every groan and every sound, both big and small.

The owl could have been around for years but just the past few she had noticed him. Other things seemed to have magnified in her mind after James' death. There were the smells. Several times, she had been convinced she smelled something burning but every time she checked, there was nothing. Just her overactive imagination, she supposed.

Gloria slid out of bed, grabbed her robe and padded to the kitchen. She started a pot of coffee, slipped her jacket over her bathrobe and then stepped out onto the porch with Mally.

The dusting of snow forecasters had predicted covered the ground. It was pretty to look at and it put her in the holiday spirit. She had remembered to ask Paul the evening before if a potluck Thanksgiving was okay with him and he told her he would leave it up to her.

His main priority was to enjoy some turkey and dressing, followed by a long nap on the couch and maybe watch a little football.

Mally, who wasn't used to the cold yet, was happy to head back into the warmth of the kitchen. She settled into her doggie bed by the door while Gloria fried a few slices of bacon, scrambled a couple eggs and then toasted some bread.

Puddles had been sleeping on the sofa but now he slunk into the kitchen and sniffed the air. Gloria cooked some extra slices of bacon and she shared it with her beloved pets before she settled in at the kitchen table with the morning paper.

Her mind zipped back and forth between the upcoming visit to Bill's place and the grocery-shopping list for turkey day. She wasn't keen on the crowded stores and planned to stock up on all the necessary supplies in advance.

She had just finished her breakfast and set her dirty dishes in the dishwasher when her phone rang. Gloria picked it up expecting Lucy or Ruth to be on the other end.

It was Gloria's daughter Jill. "Hello dear."

"Hi Mom. I just dropped the boys off at school and thought I'd give you a quick call."

Jill, her husband, Greg and grandsons, Ryan and Tyler had recently moved into a new home, with a little help from Gloria and her recent windfall. There had been a minor issue with the house before they closed and with the determination of a mother on a mission and some of Gloria's friends, it had been resolved.

Jill and her family were happy as clams in the new, spacious home. Gloria couldn't wait to stop by to see it finished and decorated for the holidays.

"Have you decided on a time for Thanksgiving Dinner?" her daughter asked.

"I'm glad you mentioned it," Gloria replied. "I was thinking about inviting Ruth, Dot and Lucy since none of them have family nearby." Or none at all she silently added.

"That's a great idea, Mom," Jill said. "That's very thoughtful of you."

The mother and daughter talked for several long moments and Gloria promised to stop by soon to check out the house.

Today, though, she had her hands full and the first thing on her list was to meet up with Ruth and Lucy!

***

Lucy was pacing back and forth in front of Ruth's van when Gloria pulled in the drive.

Gloria pulled off to the side and slid out of the driver's seat.

"I don't get a good feeling about this," Lucy warned when Gloria got close.

"Is the feeling as strong as it was the other night?" Maybe Lucy had developed a sixth sense now and Gloria should pay closer attention.

Lucy stopped abruptly. "It's different. Kind of like...I dunno a feeling that we're being watched." She shivered as she looked around.

Gloria's heart skipped a beat. In all the years the two women had been friends, this was the first time Gloria could recall Lucy saying something like that. She took it very seriously.

"Do you want to call it off?"

"But," Ruth piped up.

Gloria motioned her to be quiet. "This is your call, Lucy. After all, you're the one the police suspect." Now that she thought about it, who was to say that the police weren't keeping tabs on Lucy, even now?

Gloria narrowed her eyes and surveyed the house and surrounding yard. Maybe they *would* be walking into some sort of trap!

She tried to remember everything she'd ever watched on *Detective on the Side,* and how police set up a sting. If they thought Lucy was hiding something, wouldn't they want to keep her under surveillance...watch her every move?

Ruth snapped her fingers. "I've got a plan!" She darted up the side steps and disappeared inside. A few moments later, she motioned them in.

When they got inside the kitchen, she shut the door behind them and pulled the shade. "Stay here and out of sight," Ruth instructed.

Gloria had no idea what Ruth was up to but had to trust she had a plan, which was more than Gloria had. It seemed like they sat there forever and Gloria was getting anxious. "What..."

Tap, Tap. There was a light tap coming from the back of the house.

"Be right back." Ruth zigzagged around the table and out of sight.

"I wonder what she's up to," Lucy said.

When Ruth returned, she wasn't alone. Judith Arnett, a Belhaven local and motor mouth to boot, stepped into the kitchen.

Gloria's eyes widened at the sight of Judith. She was wearing a bright red wig on her head as she followed behind Ruth.

"Oh my goodness!" Gloria's hand flew to her mouth. "Where did that wig come from?" she gasped.

"Just some extra costume stuff I had boxed up in the basement." Ruth pointed to Lucy. "You two need to swap clothes," she said.

Lucy pointed at herself. "Me?"

"Let's go." Ruth waved them into the other room.

On the dining room table was a row of mannequin heads. On each of the heads was a different colored wig with different hair shapes and lengths. Some were short while others were long. One of the mannequins was bald. Gloria correctly guessed that the missing wig was now on Judith's head.

Gloria was dying to know where the wigs had come from. She didn't buy the "boxed up in the basement" story.

"Here." Ruth grabbed a medium length, light colored wig and handed it to Lucy. "Put this on."

Lucy stared at the wig in her hand, her mouth open. "Why, I..."

"Okay. I'll do it for you." Ruth snatched the wig from Lucy's hand and stuck it on her head. She tugged on the sides and stood back to inspect her handiwork.

"That red hair. We have to hide it." Ruth shoved her hand along Lucy's hairline as she pushed strands of red hair under the rubbery shell of the wig. "You've got some wiry hair there, Lucy," she commented.

Gloria hid a grin as Ruth circled around to work on the other side of Lucy's face.

Ruth stood back and studied Lucy. "Yep. I think this will work."

Lucy traipsed off to the bathroom. She flipped the light on and examined her new "do." She turned her head from side to side. "Not bad. I think I could pass for a blonde."

Ruth waited for Lucy to emerge from the bathroom. "Judith is the decoy. She's going to walk out of this place pretending to be you. If the cops are trailing you, they'll go after Judith instead."

"I didn't sign up for this," Judith argued.

Ruth gave her a hard stare. "You want me to tell everyone about..."

"No! I do not!" Judith cut her off. She wrinkled her nose.

Ruth narrowed her eyes as she studied Judith and Lucy critically. The women looked to be about the same size. "Time to swap clothes." She motioned at Lucy to follow her to the bedroom.

Judith headed into the bathroom and Lucy to a bedroom next door.

Lucy shut the door. Moments later, the door opened. Lucy snaked her hand around the partially closed bedroom door and handed her pants and shirt to Ruth.

Ruth took the clothes to Judith, who was waiting for her behind the bathroom door.

Next, Judith handed Ruth her blouse and slacks through the crack in the door.

Ruth took the clothes to the bedroom door. "Knock-knock. Your pretty princess attire has arrived," she teased.

The door opened a fraction. Lucy snatched the clothes from Ruth's hand and shut the door.

Gloria could hardly wait to see how they looked!

When Lucy emerged, Gloria giggled at the sight of her friend, who was now wearing a pink frock with a thick layer of ruffles along the front. Her slacks, a shiny, polyester brown, hung loosely on Lucy's thin hips and scrawny legs.

Lucy thrust her hand on her hip and pouted. "You have no sense of style, Judith."

Judith, who had emerged from the bathroom, looked none too happy with the sudden turn of events. She tugged at Lucy's plaid, flannel shirt. "You call this style? Why even Carl wouldn't wear this outfit," she declared. Carl was Judith's husband.

There were several unflattering bulges in the too tight pants but at least Judith had managed to get them on.

Ruth stood between the two warring women and extended her arms. "Now ladies." She stressed the word "*ladies*."

"So now what?" Judith snapped.

"Lucy, give Judith your car keys," Ruth commanded. "Judith will have to drive your Jeep home. We can call her later to bring it back."

"How did Judith get here?" Gloria asked.

"Carl dropped me off out back," Judith mumbled. "How do I get myself into these messes?"

Lucy plucked her keys from her purse and dropped them into Judith's outstretched hand. "Please be careful with my baby. I hope you know how to drive a stick shift," she added.

Judith's eyes widened. "A stick shift?" She narrowed her eyes and turned to Ruth. "Ruth..."

Ruth crossed her arms in front of her. "Surely you know how to drive a stick."

Judith clutched the keys in her hand. "Thirty years ago. No one drives a stick anymore!"

"I do," Lucy argued.

Judith, fed up with the entire situation, adjusted her wig, marched across the kitchen floor and stomped out the door and down the steps. The girls peeked out the window and watched as Judith hopped into Lucy's jeep.

The jeep jerked out of the drive and stalled in the middle of the road. Gloria could see Judith's lips moving and would bet the farm that she was cussing them out.

Ruth leaned over Gloria's shoulder and watched Judith. "She'll get over it," she predicted.

Finally, Judith was able to get the jeep moving forward and it lurched to the corner. Judith squealed around the corner and disappeared from sight. "I hope she's careful with Beep," Lucy whispered.

Gloria stood upright. "Beep?"

"That's my jeep's name. Beep."

Gloria thought she was the only one that named her vehicles. She turned to Ruth, the master planner. "Now what?"

"You and I head out smooth and easy, then we circle around and pick Lucy up in the alley," she said.

Lucy frowned as she glanced at the pink pumps...Judith's pink, sensible pumps that were now on her feet. "I-I've never walked in heels before."

Gloria patted her on the back. "You can do it Lucy. Think of them as barn boots with a small heel," she suggested.

Lucy took a few tentative steps, her ankles turned as she attempted to balance. "I don't know about this."

"You'll be fine," Ruth waved an arm, grabbed a cardboard box from the table and headed to the door.

Gloria followed Ruth out the front door while Lucy stumbled to the back. Lucy wasn't kidding when she said she wasn't used to heels!

Gloria hopped in the passenger seat of Ruth's van while Ruth opened the rear door and slid the box in the back. She closed the door and made her way to the driver's side. "Looks like the coast is clear," she said.

Ruth backed out of the drive, circled around the block and pulled into the alley where Lucy was hovering behind a large evergreen bush.

She slid into the back of the van, or maybe it was more like tripped into the back of the van. She yanked the door shut and crawled across the floor.

Lucy wrenched the pastel pink shoes from both feet and dropped them on the floor. "I'd rather walk on shards of glass than spend one more second in those toe pinching, heel grinding weapons of agony," she moaned dramatically.

They had just made it past the village limit sign when Ruth's cell phone beeped. Gloria glanced down at the screen. "It's Judith."

"Answer it," Ruth said.

"Hello?"

"Ruth?" Judith gasped.

"No. This is Gloria. I have you on speaker. Ruth is driving," she explained.

"Yeah. Well, I just wanted to let you know that a four-door sedan with tinted windows followed me home. They're parked across the street from my house. What should I do?"

"Stay there until I tell you to come back to my house," Ruth instructed.

"But I planned to meet some friends at Dot's for breakfast," Judith whined.

"Judith..." Ruth warned.

Silence.

"Okay, but you owe me one!"

Judith hung up before Ruth could reply.

She shrugged as she turned the corner at the stop sign. "She can be such a baby."

Lucy directed Ruth out of town, past the Montbay County line and onto a dirt road, that Gloria was certain she'd never noticed before. "Bill lives...err, lived out here?" The place was desolate.

"Yep. I think we have another quarter mile to go," Lucy guessed.

The road quickly turned into a narrow, rutted path that jostled the van and caused Gloria's stomach to feel queasy. She clutched her middle section. "I hope we're almost there."

"Turn in here." Lucy pointed to an even narrower road, which was more like a two track or dirt path.

Ruth peered through the front windshield "Are you sure?"

"Yep. This runs along the back of Bill's property. Not many people know you can get to his place from here."

This would work out perfect to stay incognito.

Ruth drove until the van couldn't move forward without taking off chunks of paint. She shifted the van in park and shut the engine off. "End of the road. Literally."

Lucy shoved her feet in Judith's shoes. "I can't believe I have to put these back on," she grumbled.

Gloria grabbed the passenger door handle. "Time to roll."

Chapter 11

The cold November morning air nipped at the tip of Gloria's nose. The dusting of snow that had covered the ground earlier had disappeared. In its place was a blanket of wet, sticky leaves along with some downed tree limbs and branches thrown in for good measure.

"This way." Lucy pointed to a row of tall pine trees. She led the way with Gloria close behind. Ruth brought up the rear with her box of goodies.

Gloria hadn't asked what all Ruth had determined was necessary for their mission. She figured she would find out soon enough.

The girls wound their way around the trees. A light breeze rustled through the trees and it made a low, moaning sound that Gloria decided sounded like, "Whoa..."

Gloria shivered involuntarily. "You sure we're headed in the right direction?" It seemed as if they were going in circles.

Lucy nodded but didn't slow her pace. "We're almost there," she promised.

Moments later, they reached a large clearing and a brick ranch house. On the front porch were a couple of old wooden ladder-back chairs. In one corner was a planter, the plant inside shriveled and limp.

Gloria stepped into the clearing and stood next to Lucy.

"Wait!" Ruth said. "We need to make sure the coast is clear."

Her eyes studied the house and then traveled upwards as she scanned the tree line. Her shoulders slumped. "It's not safe for the drone. Not sayin' it's gonna happen but I'm afraid it'll get caught in the trees."

She set the cardboard box on the ground, lifted the flaps and folded them back. Ruth peered inside the box and pulled out what looked like a small satellite dish. The base was solid black. The front part, shaped like a cone, was a frosted white color.

Ruth carefully set the device on the ground and then reached inside the box again. She pulled out a headset, slid it over the top of her head and adjusted the earpieces snugly against her ears.

With her index finger, she spun the dial on the side. Next, she flipped a small switch on the side of the dish and held a finger to her lips. "Shhh."

Gloria and Lucy watched quietly as Ruth fiddled with the headpiece. Moments later, she slid the headphones down so they rested against the nape of her neck. "The coast is clear. I heard a few birds and maybe a couple squirrels but that's all."

Gloria pointed to the cone. "Is that what I think it is?"

Ruth ran her finger along the rim of the cone. "It's a supersonic listening device. This baby can pick up noises up to 100 yards away, even inside a house." She tapped the top. "Just got this in the mail yesterday."

"I think you missed your calling." Gloria grinned. Ruth was accumulating quite an arsenal of spy equipment. "What will they think of next?"

Ruth's eyes lit. "I'm waiting on this handheld fogger device. It masks the human scent, say for example, if you were being chased by a K9 unit." She rubbed her hands together. "It should be here next week."

She went on. "My goal is to cover the five senses. I haven't been able to nail down taste." Ruth wrinkled her nose. "So far what's out there on the market hasn't worked for me. I'm waiting for something good to come along."

Gloria wondered how it "hadn't worked" for Ruth and who exactly Ruth had tested it on. She frowned. Why in the world would Ruth need to try to hide her scent and avoid the police?

Gloria handed her the portable monitor. That was a question to save for another day. First things first.

Ruth set the monitor and headphones inside the box and closed the lid. "I'll pick this up on our way out."

Lucy waved them forward. When they reached the front porch steps, she came to an abrupt halt and lowered her head. Her hand shook as she reached for the knob.

Gloria put a hand on Lucy's shoulder. "Are you sure you're ready for this?"

Lucy nodded. "Yeah. Bill wouldn't want me to have to go through this, no matter how badly our relationship ended."

Lucy pulled a key from her front pocket. She inserted the key in the lock and turned. It wouldn't budge. "Uh-oh. It doesn't work." She pulled the key back out.

"Here, let me try." Gloria took the key from Lucy and slipped it inside the deadbolt. She jiggled it back and forth and finally, it turned. "It was just a little sticky."

The door creaked loudly as Gloria gingerly pushed it open and stepped inside. Lucy was right behind her. Ruth brought up the rear.

The house smelled musty.

Gloria wrinkled her nose. "Do you smell that?"

Ruth nodded. "Yeah. Smells damp."

Gloria took a tentative step forward. The floorboard creaked and Lucy jumped. She pressed a hand to her chest. "Oh my gosh!"

Gloria took another step. The hair on the back of her neck bristled.

A sudden, muffled thump echoed through the house.

"Wh-what was that?" Lucy whispered.

"It sounded like it was coming from the kitchen," Gloria murmured. She rubbed her sweaty palms on the top of her jeans. Should they high tail it out of there or press on to the kitchen?

They had come too far to turn back now. She took a firm step forward, determined to see this mission through, no matter what the outcome!

They finished crossing the living room floor.

Gloria stopped in the doorway that led to the kitchen. The kitchen was modern and spacious. She wasn't sure what she expected since Bill was pure outdoorsman. Maybe a faucet shaped like a grizzly bear.

The kitchen was far from rustic. In fact, it was a little too modern for Gloria's own taste with its sleek lines and flat cabinets. The walls were a light gray.

The backsplash a pale green subway tile. "This wasn't at all what I expected."

Lucy had to agree. "Yeah. He was kind of a stickler for cleanliness."

A small movement over the kitchen sink caught Ruth's eye. "The kitchen window – it's open."

Sure enough, the window above the kitchen sink was wide open.

Lucy slipped past Gloria and approached the sink. She leaned across the sink, put both hands on the sill, pulled down and snapped the lock in place. "Bill would never have left the window open."

Gloria stepped over to the sliding glass door and peered out. "You think someone else was in here?" It was possible that someone in Bill's family had opened the window and forgot to close it before they left.

She glanced down at the expensive oak floors. Humidity and moisture had warped several of the boards. Gloria rubbed her shoe over the bumpy surface. "What a shame. These will have to be fixed."

Lucy led them from the kitchen, across the dining area and into the hall. "Bill used the first bedroom for storage and the second one was his office."

Lucy grasped the handle on the first door they came to. She turned the knob and pushed the door open.

Gloria peeked over Lucy's shoulder and gasped when she looked inside. The room was in shambles. In one corner were floor-to-ceiling boxes. Strewn across the floor were piles of wrinkled clothes. The closet doors were wide open and shoved off to one side was a row of wire hangers.

Pushed up against the far wall was a black futon. On top of the futon was a navy blue sleeping bag, unzipped. It looked as if someone had been sleeping on it.

A camo-patterned strip of material caught Gloria's eye. She stepped over to the bed, reached underneath and tugged on it. It was a backpack. Something a hunter or possibly a college student might use to carry supplies.

Gloria held the backpack in her hand. "You said this room was for storage? It looks like someone was sleeping in here."

Lucy frowned. "Yeah. Last time I was here, Bill used the room for storage. I've never seen that futon before."

Did that mean that someone had been living with Bill? Gloria vaguely recalled that Bill had divorced his first wife years ago and that they had had two daughters. She couldn't remember their names. "What about Bill's daughters?"

Lucy scrunched up her nose. "One of them lives in Wisconsin and the other one lives overseas where her husband is stationed in the military."

It was possible they had just arrived in town and were staying at Bill's place. If that were the case, there would be suitcases and other travel bags.

Gloria shoved the backpack back under the bed and followed Lucy into the hall.

Lucy closed the door behind them and made her way to the room across the hall. The door was open and Gloria peeked inside. The room was empty.

There was nothing inside…not a stick of furniture, not a picture on the wall. Nothing.

"That's odd. This used to be Bill's office. It was full of office furniture."

If Bill had removed everything from the room, what had he done with it?

The trio passed by a hall bath on their way to the master bedroom at the end. Double doors opened to the spacious master suite. The room was clean, the bed made. A door on the far end led to a small screened-in porch.

Gloria glanced out the window. Centered against one wall was a white wicker loveseat with navy blue cushions. A matching wicker table sat next to it. On top of the wicker table was an ashtray.

Lucy opened the door and stepped out onto the porch. She pointed at the ashtray. "Huh. That's odd. Bill quit smoking years ago. In fact, he hated the smell."

The girls finished their inspection of the master bedroom and adjoining bath.

They retraced their steps as they made their way to the end of the hall. At the end of the hall was an open staircase leading down to the basement. Although the steps were carpeted, they still creaked – loudly - when the girls stepped on them.

Gloria wondered how a house that was only a few years old could have so many creaks and groans.

At the bottom of the steps, Lucy fumbled with the light switch on the wall. A bare bulb in the center of the ceiling cast a dim glow and illuminated the open space. The room was empty except for a desk, chair, bookcase and file cabinet squeezed against the far wall.

Gloria glanced around. The basement was small, much smaller than she thought it would be for a house that large. "This is it?" she asked.

Lucy nodded. "Yep. For some reason, Bill didn't see the need for a large basement. He said the only thing basements were good for was storing junk. He always said if he did anything, he'd build a bomb shelter."

She pointed to the wall. "There is his office equipment."

Gloria frowned. Why would Bill move his office downstairs and into a dark, dreary basement instead of leaving it upstairs in a bright, airy bedroom? It didn't make sense.

Lucy slipped into the chair and settled in behind the desk. She turned the computer on and waited until the login screen appeared. "I'm not sure if Bill's password is the same." Lucy clicked a few of the keys and hit enter. An error message appeared.

She tried again, and again she got an error message. "Nope. He must have changed it." She tried to guess the password but nothing worked. Finally, it locked her out. "I have no idea what his password is."

While Lucy worked on the computer, Ruth searched the bookcase and Gloria rifled through the cabinets. Nothing popped up as suspicious. There were folders for receipts, bills and other important papers.

Not once did Gloria's internal radar go up. She shut the cabinet door and took a step back. Ruth joined her. "The place is clean."

"Looks like we just wasted our time." Lucy pushed the chair back. Her fingers pressed against a desk calendar and it shifted forward. The corner of a small slip of paper appeared.

Lucy reached down and pulled on the paper. "What's this?" She flipped the piece over and squinted at the words scribbled on the back.

"12 Grand Marais Drive, Detroit, MI 49962"

A smudge of what appeared to be blood stained the corner.

"I wonder if that's Bill's blood." Gloria's stomach churned at the thought.

"Let me get a plastic baggie so we can take it with us." Lucy darted up the stairs without waiting for a reply.

She returned moments later. Using the corner of the clear, plastic bag, she slid the slip of paper inside and pulled the tab across the top to seal it shut.

They finished their search of the basement and utility room, which turned up nothing. At least they had something…the small slip of paper.

Disappointed, the trio trudged up the stairs. Ruth was the last one out and she flipped the light switch on her way up.

The women retraced their steps through the living room and exited through the front door. Lucy glanced toward the kitchen. "Do you think whoever has been inside the house will notice that we closed the window?"

Gloria's brows formed a "V." True...if someone was staying in the house, there was a good chance they would notice. Then again, if they didn't close the window and the house was vacant, wild animals and the elements would damage much more than a section of the kitchen floor.

When they reached the edge of the yard, Ruth stopped to pick up her surveillance equipment. Gloria and Ruth followed behind Lucy as they zigzagged through the pine trees.

The tops of the trees began to bend and sway as the wind picked up. The wind whistled through the treetops and it began to rain.

The freezing rain pelted their faces and clothes. The girls picked up the pace in an attempt to outrun the sudden storm.

By the time they reached the van, they were soaking wet.

When they were safely inside the van, Ruth switched the motor on, turned the center dial to heat and cranked it all the way up. "That was fun."

Warm air blasted from the ducts and Gloria stuck her hands in front of the warm air. "I'm not sure I'm ready for winter," she admitted. She loved fall and loved having a white Christmas to put her in the holiday spirit but after New Year's, the winter weather was for the birds...or the outdoor enthusiasts.

Lucy wiped her forehead with one of the ruffles from the front of Judith's fancy pink blouse. "Since Paul is retiring, maybe you guys can become snowbirds. You know, spend the winter months somewhere warm like Florida."

Lucy leaned forward in her seat. "I'll be the first one to come visit!" she promised.

Gloria's sister, Liz and her best friend, Frances, had recently moved to Florida. It was a thought. The idea of warm, sunny weather was appealing. "We might just do that," Gloria answered.

"First, we have to get out of the woods, literally," Ruth grimaced. She shifted the van into reverse and slowly backed out of the woods.

Sharp branches scraped the windows and the sides of the van. Gloria cringed each time a branch scraped the side. This had been her idea and she would never forgive herself if Ruth's van were damaged during one of her investigations.

Finally, they reached the main road and turned toward home.

Gloria hoped that Andrea and Margaret had better luck with the mysterious gun rep, Maxim, than they had searching Bill's house.

Chapter 12

Ruth handed Gloria her cell phone. "Call Judith and let her know we're on the way."

Gloria dialed the number and switched it to speaker-mode.

Judith picked up on first ring. "Please tell me you're on your way back."

Gloria smiled wickedly. "We're on our way back."

"Good!" Judith gasped through the line. "These clothes are downright itchy. Lucy must wash her clothes in poison ivy."

"I do not!" Lucy leaned forward in her seat. "I use only all natural ingredients."

"I'll be waiting in the drive." Judith hung up before Ruth could reply.

Ruth dropped Lucy off one street over, circled around the block and pulled into her drive.

Judith, true to her word, was waiting for them. She swung the jeep door open and hopped out of the driver's seat. She didn't look at all happy as she trudged up the drive, scratching at her arms, her stomach and her neck as she walked.

Gloria could see large red welts covering her skin. "Wow! That looks bad," she commented.

The women traipsed up the steps and into the house. Ruth made her way to the back door to let Lucy in.

The two women swapped clothes. Lucy handed Judith her shoes. "Those are the most uncomfortable shoes I have ever worn."

Judith grabbed the shoes. "Can't be any worse than your clothes," she snapped.

Judith shoved her foot into the shoe and pointed at Ruth. "I've paid my dues and upheld my end of the bargain."

Ruth nodded solemnly. "Yes, you have Judith and I thank you for your cooperation."

Judith snatched her purse off the table, turned on her heels and stomped out the door, slamming the door shut behind her.

Lucy grinned. "I would give anything to know what Ruth had on her to make her agree to the swap."

They watched Judith hustle down the sidewalk and disappear around the corner.

Ruth shook her head. "No can do. Judith held up her end of the bargain and I need to uphold mine."

Lucy reached into her purse and pulled out the plastic bag with the small piece of paper inside. "Do you have time to check this out?"

Ruth glanced at the clock on the wall. It was almost lunchtime. "Yeah. Kenny isn't expecting me to come in until after lunch."

She waved the girls past the small eat-in area and down the narrow hall off to one side. She stopped in front of the first door and they followed her inside.

The room was dark and the curtain drawn tight with nary a sliver of light coming in.

Ruth shuffled over to the other side of the room and switched on a small desk lamp that sat on top of the desk.

Gloria had never been in the back of Ruth's house. She'd only seen the kitchen, dining and living room.

If Gloria had an inkling that Ruth was obsessed with surveillance equipment, she was now 100% convinced of the fact.

The room was floor-to-ceiling monitors. Every square inch of wall space was filled with electronic gadgets and boxes.

A giant map of Michigan covered one entire wall. Circled in bright red pen was the Town of Belhaven.

Round, color-coated tacks dotted the map. Gloria reached into her purse, slipped on her reading glasses and peered at the map. "What do all those colored dots represent?"

"Uh, just a little map for tracking different post offices," Ruth explained.

Gloria wasn't convinced. Down in the lower right hand cover was a legend. She bent down and leaned in.

"That is of no interest to you," Ruth blurted out. "We have more important things to worry about!"

Gloria was itching to find out what the colored dots and legend meant, but she didn't want to put Ruth on the spot.

"You're right." Gloria looked longingly at the map and then turned her attention to Ruth. "We need to get down to business."

Ruth slid into the seat at the desk. She wiggled the mouse until the computer came to life.

Lucy read the address on the small sheet of paper.

Ruth typed in the address and clicked the "search" button. Several results popped up...all of them listing the same place: East Michigan Swap and Shop, a Detroit area gun shop that took guns in trade and bought used guns.

What did that mean? Obviously, it meant something to Bill...or whoever was using Bill's computer. But why Detroit? It was almost 200 miles away!

***

Gloria climbed in Annabelle and started for home. She made a last minute decision to stop at Nails and Knobs, Brian Sellers' hardware store.

The parking lot was full. Gloria turned down a side street and parked behind the building.

Brian had recently painted the hardware store, along with the small pharmacy and grocery store...stores that he also owned. All three buildings now matched and it somehow helped make the cozy Town of Belhaven appear uniform and even quainter.

She made her way inside and walked to the back of the store. Brian was waiting on a customer. He smiled when he caught a glimpse of Gloria.

Gloria waited off to one side while Brian rang up the customer's purchases. After the customer left, she wound her way around the light fixtures and garden hoses and over to the counter.

She set her purse on the edge of the counter and hopped up on one of the barstools. Brian reached behind him for the pot of coffee and a cup. "I was beginning to think you were avoiding me," he teased.

"Me? Avoid you?" Gloria snorted. "More like the other way around." It was true. She hadn't seen much of Brian lately.

He had taken a brief vacation to visit his father, who had suffered a minor stroke. Other than seeing him at Andrea's the other day, it had been quite some time since they'd had a chance to chat.

He slid the piping hot cup of coffee across the counter and then leaned both elbows on top. "Doing a little sleuthing this morning?" he guessed.

Gloria lifted the coffee cup to her lips and took a sip. "How did you know?"

"I stopped by the post office to mail some packages and Ruth was MIA. When I asked Kenny what happened to her, he mumbled something about an unexpected emergency so I put two and two together and figured you two were trying to crack Lucy's case."

Gloria fiddled with the handle of the mug. "What do you think?"

Brian shrugged his shoulders. "Judging by the gossip around town and what I've been told, it looks like someone is trying to frame Lucy."

"That's what I think," Gloria agreed. "We have some suspects but nothing solid. No smoking gun so-to-speak."

She listed the suspects and gave Brian a brief rundown of each of their motives.

"I think Bill rejected that Barbara woman. Maybe she went crazy with jealousy and murdered him," she theorized.

She went on. "Next is the brother, Randy. One of the employees told me that Bill and his brother had a huge blowout a couple days before his death."

Gloria shifted in her chair. "Last, but not least, is the gun dealer that Bill seemed to be somewhat intimidated by." That reminded her she needed to do a little snooping around on him once she got a report back on Andrea and Margaret's findings.

"What does Lucy think?" Brian asked. She knew Bill better than the rest of them combined.

"Lucy is in a haze." Not that Gloria could blame her. This whole thing reeked of a set up. Someone who was close to Bill knew that Lucy would be a prime suspect. She remembered the employee, Zeke, who seemed all too willing to throw everyone else on the tracks.

"I should go." Gloria glanced at her watch and slid off the barstool. "Thanks for the coffee."

Brian reached for the empty coffee cup. "How are the wedding plans going?"

The wedding plans weren't "going" anywhere. They were almost at a standstill. Not that there was much to do at this point...the invitations had been sent, the wedding party and location ready to go, along with the food. The only thing left to do was pick out a dress and flowers.

"It's right on track. Speaking of that, are you and Andrea ever going to settle down?" Gloria blurted out.

"Now that you mention it." Brian opened the cabinet drawer behind him, reached inside and pulled out a small box. "What do you think?"

Gloria smiled. "Well, I know that this box isn't for me."

Brian and Paul had tricked Gloria into thinking the engagement ring Paul had bought for her was one that Brian intended to give to Andrea. Paul had been so nervous about her liking the ring, that he had her give her "seal of approval," in a roundabout way.

Brian lifted the cover off the box and pulled out a second box, covered in white velvet.   He lifted the lid and held it out. A large, marquise cut diamond ring was nestled inside.

Gloria picked up the box and set it in the palm of her hand. "Oh Brian. This ring is beautiful!" She shifted her gaze and stared at Brian. "When…"

Brian grinned. "I was thinking of taking her on a romantic carriage ride in downtown Grand Rapids and popping the question."

"How romantic," Gloria gushed. She handed the ring back and clapped her hands. "Oooh! I hope I can keep my mouth shut. This is so exciting," she babbled.

"You better keep quiet or we won't make you the godmother of our children," he threatened.

"Godmother? Oh my gosh!" Her hand flew to her chest.

The front bell tinkled and an elderly couple that Gloria vaguely recognized made their way to the back.

Brian closed the lid on the box, popped it back inside the outer box and then slipped it into the drawer. He made a zipping motion across his lips.

"I promise." Gloria zipped her own lips. "I better go." With a spring in her step, Gloria headed down the center aisle and out onto the sidewalk.

The day had started out rough around the edges, but Brian's exciting news made Gloria want to explode into a million tiny pieces. She could hardly wait to tell someone, anyone, but she knew she couldn't.

Chapter 13

Andrea pulled her truck into the parking lot, eased into an empty spot and shut the engine off. The place was deader than a doornail. The only other vehicle in the parking lot was a four-door late model sedan. She wondered if it belonged to the gun dealer...

A shiver of fear raced down her back. Was this gun dealer also a killer? Andrea cast a wary glance toward the store. It was possible that any of the employees inside the store could be Bill's murderer.

Andrea grabbed the edges of her jacket and pulled them tight. "I'm a little nervous!"

Margaret shifted her purse on her shoulder. "Yeah. I get a bad feeling about this place." Her eyes wandered around the empty parking lot. She had a nagging feeling that they were being set up. She made a vow to stop watching so many creepy movies.

The store bell tinkled as Andrea pushed on the door and the women stepped into the shop. Margaret followed Andrea to the counter in the back.

A young man that Andrea vaguely remembered from the day before approached them. "Can I help you?"

Andrea set her handbag on the edge of the counter. "Yes. We were in here yesterday talking to…"

"Barbara," Margaret prompted.

"Barbara," Andrea continued, "and she said the Kahr® handgun rep would be here this morning."

The young man with the jet-black hair nodded. "Yep. He's talking to one of the owners now."

Margaret glanced at his nametag: *Zeke*. She frowned. "I thought the owner recently died."

Zeke shook his head. "Yeah. He did." Zeke left it at that and quickly changed the subject.

"I'll go get Mr. Maxim."

He opened a door that led to the back and disappeared from sight. "That's interesting," Andrea muttered under her breath.

Zeke returned. With him was a bald-headed man. "This is Artie Maxim, our Kahr® representative."

The man sported a gray goatee and wore a brown trench coat that brushed against the floor. It reminded Andrea of a coat killers wore while walking down a dark alley in the dead of night, stalking their prey.

Andrea mentally shook her head to clear the thought. There was nothing odd about a man wearing a trench coat on a drizzly November morning. "Yes. We were here yesterday and one of the guns my mother and I wanted to take a look at was not in stock."

He nodded. "Barbara left a note. It was a Kahr®." He tapped his finger on the glass case where there was an empty spot. "There's only one model left. Have you seen it?"

He motioned for Zeke to unlock the cabinet.

Zeke shoved his hands in his front pockets. "Uh. I don't have a key to this case. Barbara is the only one who has the key and she's not here," he said.

"What about Randy? Maxim frowned.

"Nope. Not even Randy. We're gonna get another key made but haven't gotten around to it yet."

Andrea remembered Barbara telling them yesterday that the Kahr® gun, identical to the one that had killed Bill and the same one that Lucy had at home, had come up missing from the case.

Maxim folded his hands in front of him. "How do customers look at guns if there's no key to unlock the case?"

"They don't," Zeke replied. "I mean, it's only been a month or so. It wasn't a problem before. Bill had a key and Barbara had a key. One of them was always working."

"What about Bill's key?" Andrea couldn't help asking the question.

Zeke nodded. "Yeah. We checked his key ring and for some reason, it's missing. Just like the model gun that killed him."

***

"That is no way to run a business!" Maxim whacked his open palm on the counter. "I could be losing thousands of dollars in commission with this shoddily run operation," he fumed.

Andrea shrank back. Maxim was turning out to be as sinister as she had suspected. She could even imagine him taking Bill out back and shooting him. But where was the motive? She wondered if Gloria had had a chance to do a little preliminary research on him yet.

He narrowed his eyes and scowled. "Never mind."

Maxim shifted the duffel bag he was holding. He reached inside the bag and lifted out a lumpy roll of canvas. He set the canvas on the glass top and unfolded it.

Inside the canvas was a whole arsenal of guns. The girls spent the next hour learning about each weapon and their pros and cons. To Andrea it was fascinating. It was boring Margaret to tears.

Lucy would have loved it.

After Maxim explained each weapon in detail, Andrea took his card and promised to discuss which one would work best with her mother.

The women thanked Maxim and Zeke for their time and wandered out of the store.

The skies had opened up and hard rain, almost a hail, pelted the truck. "I hope the roads haven't started icing over yet," Andrea fretted. The truck was a dream to drive except when it came to ice. Andrea hated driving on ice.

Andrea fumbled around inside her bag, pulled out her keys and unlocked the truck doors. The girls hurriedly climbed inside and yanked the doors shut.

Andrea backed the truck around, pulled out of the drive and onto the main road.

The wind picked up and the rain turned into freezing rain. She slowed the truck, gripped the wheel and focused on the road. It was going to be a white-knuckle drive home.

Finally, she turned the truck onto a side road and let out the breath she had been holding. She could feel the truck slide as they rounded the corner.

Margaret sat quietly in the passenger seat. She didn't want to distract Andrea, who focused all her attention on the road in front of her.

Instead, Margaret prayed a silent prayer they would make it home safely.

Suddenly, a car that had been following Andrea's truck, a little too close in Margaret's opinion, zipped around them and attempted to pass on a double yellow line.

"Jerk!" Andrea muttered. She took her foot off the gas so that the car could get by. The red car, a beat up two door, rusting around the bottom, started to lose control and fishtail in front of them.

Andrea instinctively hit the brakes, which caused the truck to lose control on the ice. The vehicle spun in a wide circle and hit the edge of the gravel road where it gained a little traction.

It was too late. The front tire bounced off a large rock causing the vehicle to shift sideways. When the truck stopped spinning, the girls were smack dab in the middle of an open field, facing the opposite direction.

The car that had caused them to spin out was long gone.

Andrea sucked in a breath and put her forehead on the steering wheel.

Margaret reached over and patted her arm. "Good job, Andrea," she said.

Andrea opened her eyes and lifted her head. "Thanks. What a jerk!" she fumed.

She looked around the open field. "Let's see if I can get the truck back on the road." Andrea pressed a button on the dashboard and switched the truck to four-wheel drive. She shifted the truck into reverse and pressed lightly on the gas pedal.

The truck made a sudden jerking motion as it began to move backward. They made it about halfway out of the field when the truck began to sink in the soft dirt.

"Oh no!" Andrea pressed the gas pedal harder, which caused the vehicle to sink further into the field.

"Try rocking it," Margaret suggested. She knew that trick sometimes worked with a manual transmission. She wasn't sure if it would work with an automatic.

Andrea shifted the gears from drive to reverse several times. They went nowhere, except maybe a little deeper in the mud.

She rolled down the window and stuck her head out as she inspected the tires. "This isn't going to work. We'll have to call a tow truck."

"Give Gus a call," Margaret suggested. "He can pull us out." "Gus" was Gus Smith, a Belhaven resident who owned a small towing and automotive shop.

"Good idea." Andrea pulled her cell phone from her purse. She pressed the "on" button, switched to search mode and typed in "G.S. Towing and Automotive, Belhaven, Michigan." When she found the number, she pressed the call button.

Thankfully, Gus picked up on the second ring. Andrea explained her – their - situation and Gus told her was on his way.

Andrea disconnected the line and slumped down in the driver's seat. "This sucks. I wish I could get my hands on that driver!"

Gus showed up half an hour later. He waded across the mucky field and approached the driver's side door.

Andrea rolled down the window.

"You dug yourself a hole," he observed.

"Yeah," Andrea groaned. "Some moron decided to not only pass on a double yellow line but on an icy road. When he started to spin out in front of me, I hit the brakes and here we are."

Gus nodded. "Yeah. It takes some of these blockheads a while to figure out the roads are slippery."

He went on. "Let me get you hooked up."

Gus lumbered back to his wrecker. He unwound a long cable from the back of his wrecker. On the end of the cable were two long hooks. He hooked the large metal hooks to the underneath of her truck and then climbed behind the wheel of his tow truck.

The cable slowly retracted as the winch wound the cable around the metal cylinder.

Andrea let out a sigh of relief as the truck began to inch its way out of the field and back onto the road.

When the truck was safely off to the side and parked in the gravel, she climbed out of the truck and waited while Gus removed the hooks. "Thank you, Gus. How much do I owe you?"

Gus fastened the hooks on the back of the wrecker. "You get the family discount," he teased. "Twenty-five bucks. You can just meet me back at the shop. I forgot to bring my portable card scanner."

Andrea frowned. "That seems too cheap, Gus. I think you should charge me more."

Gus snorted. "Most people think I charge too much." He shrugged. "Okay. Forty bucks."

"Deal. I'll meet you back at your place." She climbed in the driver's seat and fastened her seatbelt.

They followed Gus to his shop and both women met him at the door and followed him inside.

Andrea glanced back at her truck and frowned. A thick layer of mud covered the lower half of her driver's side door, the trim and the running boards. "Great. I guess our next stop will be the car wash."

They stepped inside the repair shop and over to the small counter where Gus was writing up a ticket. "Nice truck," he commented as he handed her a receipt and took her card to swipe it through his credit card machine.

When he had finished processing the transaction, Andrea shoved her card back inside her wallet and glanced at Margaret. There was a red bump on the side of her forehead. "Margaret, did you bump your head?"

Margaret touched her forehead. "Yeah. I think I might have."

Andrea leaned in for a closer inspection. "I think that is going to bruise. I am so sorry."

Margaret shook her head. "It's not your fault, Andrea. You didn't cause the accident. I'll be fine," she reassured her young friend.

Andrea felt terrible. "Let's stop at Dot's and get a bag of ice."

Andrea hopped in the driver's seat and Margaret slid into the passenger seat. She backed out of the parking out and turned the truck toward Main Street.

Thankfully, there was an empty parking spot right out front. Andrea pulled the truck into the empty spot and shut the engine off.

Andrea waited for Margaret near the front of the truck. "Do you feel dizzy? Light headed?"

Margaret waved her hand and opened the door to the restaurant. "I'm fine. It's just a little bump."

"What if it's a concussion?" Andrea fretted.

"Who has a concussion?" Dot rushed over. "Oh gosh!" A large lump had begun to swell on Margaret's forehead. "You should sit down."

Dot led Margaret to a chair in the back. "Ray! Grab a bag of ice!" she hollered into the kitchen. She turned to the girls. "What happened?"

Andrea shifted her purse. "We ditched the truck after some moron tried to go around us on the slippery roads."

She slid into the seat next to Margaret and studied the swelling. "I am so sorry Margaret," she whispered. "I wish it had been me, not you."

"Nonsense," Margaret waved her hand. "You two are making too much of a fuss over me. I'll be fine."

Ray made his way over to the trio. He handed the bag of ice and a clean, dry rag to Margaret. "How'd you get that goose egg?"

Andrea frowned. "We had a run in with the ditch and Margaret bumped her noggin."

Margaret covered the bag of ice with the clean rag and placed it against her forehead. "It feels better already."

Dot changed the subject. "Well? How did it go at the store? Did you find anything out?"

Andrea explained what had happened. "I don't know what to think. I'm not ruling out Barbara, who is the only employee with the key, or Bill's brother, Randy." She crossed her arms in front of her and leaned back in the chair. "Who knows? Maybe even the gun rep was involved."

Dot glanced at her watch. "Gloria and the rest of the girls should be here anytime. I wonder if they found anything over at Bill's house."

Andrea and Margaret ordered hot tea and a plate of decadent desserts. They munched on the sweet treats and discussed the case. This was the first time that Gloria had sent them out on their own covert operation and it was exciting to be right in the middle of the investigation.

Margaret reached for a strawberry donut and nibbled on the outer ring. "This is delicious. I've never tasted a strawberry donut. Here. Try this." She broke off a piece and handed it to Andrea.

Andrea bit into the donut. "Wow! This is so good. Are these new?"

Dot nodded. "Yep. I've been experimenting with strawberries for a while and think I finally got the recipe right."

"It's a winner." Andrea popped the last of the shared donut in her mouth.

She stared at the door anxiously. "I wish Gloria would hurry up. I'm dying to know what happened."

Margaret nodded and lifted her teacup to take a sip. The cup slipped out of her hand and clattered against the saucer. She put a hand to her head. "I'm not feeling good." She slumped over in the chair and laid her head on the table in front of her.

Chapter 14

Andrea shot out of her seat. "Margaret!" She shook her arm gently. Margaret didn't respond.

"Call 911!" Andrea shrieked to no one in particular. "Margaret. Margaret! Can you hear me?" Her eyes frantically searched the restaurant. "Does anyone here have medical training?"

A young woman rushed to Margaret's side. "I'm a nurse." The woman dropped to her knees and gently turned Margaret's head. Next, she placed her cheek close to Margaret's mouth and then glanced at Margaret's chest. "She appears to be breathing."

Margaret jerked her head. "I'm just a little dizzy," she mumbled. Her words were slurred and it was difficult to understand what she had said.

"We're going to move you into a more comfortable position." The woman placed a hand under each of Margaret's arms and gently pulled.

Andrea wrapped her arms around Margaret's middle. The women lowered Margaret to the floor of the restaurant and then placed her on her side.

The nurse tipped Margaret's head to ensure her neck and windpipe were in an unobstructed position. The young brunette glanced at Andrea. "What happened?"

"She bumped her head a short time ago when we slid into the ditch," Andrea explained.

Margaret placed a hand on the side of her head. "I'll be fine. I just need to go home and rest," she protested.

The fire department arrived moments later, followed by an ambulance. Despite her protests, paramedics gently lifted Margaret onto a gurney and wheeled her toward the front door.

The gurney was on its way out the door as Gloria, Ruth and Lucy were on their way in. Gloria did an about face when she saw Margaret on the gurney. "What in the world..."

"We had a small accident." Tears began to burn the back of Andrea's eyes. "Margaret hit her head on the passenger side window of my truck. She insists that she's fine but she's not."

Dot, Ruth, Gloria, Lucy and Andrea all climbed into Ruth's van.

Gloria promptly called Don, Margaret's husband, to let him know that Margaret was on the way to the hospital. She left a message on his cell phone and another on the home phone.

They followed the ambulance to Green Springs Memorial Hospital, the small community hospital in nearby Green Springs.

On the way, Andrea explained what had happened at Bill's shop and then told them about the reckless driver who had caused them to spin off into the ditch.

"Stupid jerk. I wish I could get my hands on the driver," Andrea clenched her fists in her lap. "I'd wring their sorry neck!"

When they reached the ER entrance, the girls all climbed out of the van while Ruth drove off to find a parking spot.

They found a small cluster of chairs off in the corner of the lobby and settled in to wait for a doctor to come out.

Don arrived shortly after. The girls briefly explained what had happened and Don, accompanied by a nurse, strode down the hall in search of his wife.

Gloria watched until he disappeared from sight. "Let's pray."

The girls gathered in a small circle and held hands while Gloria prayed. "Lord, we lift up our friend, Margaret. We know that You are the God of healing and we ask that You heal Margaret's body and if there is something wrong, the doctors are able to find it right away. Thank you. In Jesus' name, we pray. Amen."

Gloria felt a sense of peace as she lifted her head. Margaret was in safe hands…God's hands.

Time passed slowly. Finally, Don emerged from the back. The girls rushed forward and crowded around.

"What did the doctors say?" Andrea asked.

Don rubbed his forehead. "She has a mild concussion and seems highly disoriented so they want to keep her overnight, just to be safe."

He went on. "I have to run home and pick up a few things for Margaret."

"I'll stay," Gloria offered.

Dot needed to get back to the restaurant. Ruth needed to get back to the post office. That left Andrea, Gloria and Lucy.

"Why don't I have Ruth drop me off at my truck and then I can come back to cover the shift," Andrea suggested.

They agreed that Andrea and Gloria would take the first shift and then a little later, Don would return to spend the night by his wife's side. "Call me immediately if anything changes," Don said before he headed out the double sliding doors.

Gloria promised she would. The rest of the girls promised to check in later and Gloria made her way to Margaret's hospital room.

She tiptoed to the edge of the door and peeked around the corner. Her heart sank when she saw her friend's still body covered in sterile hospital sheets.

Margaret propped herself up on one elbow when Gloria stepped inside the room. "Lucky you. You get babysitting duty," Margaret joked.

Gloria slid onto the hard, plastic chair that was next to the bed. "I wouldn't want to be anywhere else."

Margaret eased back down and shifted on the mattress. "I don't know why I have to stay here. Other than a little dizziness, I feel great."

"Better safe than sorry," Gloria said. She changed the subject. "I heard that you and Andrea had a successful trip to Four Seasons Sporting Goods."

Margaret ran a hand through her hair. "Yeah, it was great except for the accident," Margaret quipped. "What did you find out?"

Gloria told her about Ruth's handy dandy listening device, how they suspected someone had been living inside the house and might still be there.

She told her about the small slip of paper with a Detroit address handwritten on it and that there appeared to be a spot of blood on the edge. "It's a gun shop in Detroit."

Gloria pulled her notepad and pen from her purse. She flipped the pad of paper open and clicked the button on the pen. "We can work on the list of suspects and motives." She glanced up from the pad. "Unless you would rather rest."

"What I'd rather do is leave," Margaret grumbled. "Working the case will take my mind off this place."

"Good." Gloria nodded. "So first on the list is Randy, Bill's brother. The two had been fighting days before Bill's death and now Randy is acting like he owns the place."

"Check," Margaret agreed.

Gloria scribbled his name at the top of the notepad. "Next is Barbara, the worker that Bill didn't seem to care for but ended up dating after Lucy and he broke up. She's the only one who has a key to the gun cabinet. The case where the gun went missing and the same model that killed Bill."

"Yep," Margaret nodded.

"Then we have this Maxim, the sales guy who had access to that type of gun. Bill didn't care for him and on top of that, he hits the suspicion radar."

Margaret shivered and pulled the blanket closer. "Yeah. He was an interesting fellow, for sure. Very cagey."

Gloria tapped the end of the pen on top of the pad of paper. "Maybe Bill caught him doing something he shouldn't have been…like selling guns on the black market," she theorized.

"It's possible," Margaret agreed. "What about that young man that works at the store?"

"Zeke," Gloria said. "Yeah. He told me Bill was suspicious of all his employees and had asked Zeke to keep an eye on things when he wasn't at the store." Of course, that was Zeke's version. Bill was no longer around to corroborate the story.

"What about the funeral? I always heard that killers love to attend the funerals of their victims. They get some kind of buzz from being there." Margaret pointed out.

"True," Gloria hadn't thought about that. She wondered if Lucy would go. She hadn't been charged with Bill's murder, only questioned. "I'll check with Lucy later. I wonder when visitation or funeral services will be held."

Gloria popped out of her chair. "I bet it's listed in the local paper. I'll be right back." Gloria darted out of the hospital room and sped down the gleaming hospital corridor.

She remembered seeing a small gift shop on the first floor.

When she got to the gift shop, she was relieved to find the shop was open.

Gloria stepped inside and made a beeline for the stack of newspapers near the entrance.

She was surprised at the variety of items the store stocked. Gloria headed for the checkout counter and then circled back to pick up a bouquet of fresh flowers to take to Margaret.

After she paid for her items, she stopped by the hospital cafeteria where she grabbed a couple chicken salad sandwiches and two bags of potato chips.

Gloria juggled her purchases as she made her way back upstairs to Margaret's room. On the way to the room, she stopped at the nurse's station to make sure it was okay for Margaret to eat the food she had just purchased.

Margaret had dozed off and was startled by the sound of Gloria setting the vase of flowers on the bedside tray. "Oh! You took so long, I got sleepy."

Margaret rubbed her eyes and stared at the flowers. "Gloria! Now why did you do that?" she scolded.

"Because this place needs a splash of color." She glanced around. "Why do hospital rooms have to be so stark? A little color goes a long way."

Gloria placed a bag of food on the tray in front of Margaret. "This is for you in case you're hungry."

Margaret reached for the bag. "I'm starving. All I had were some donuts at Dot's."

The girls unwrapped their sandwiches, bowed their heads to pray and then bit into the food. It wasn't gourmet but it was more than edible and Gloria quickly devoured her sandwich. She opened the bag of chips and then unfolded the newspaper.

Bill's murder was no longer on the front page. It was three pages in. Gloria slid her reading glasses on and brought the paper close to her face. "Bingo! I found something." She leaned in to read the article.

"They're having a candlelight vigil tonight. It starts at 7:00 p.m."

She lowered the paper and gazed at Margaret. She was on the fence about mentioning it to Lucy. "Should I tell Lucy?"

Margaret shrugged and then popped a chip in her mouth. "Let Lucy decide. I'm sure she already knows about it."

True. Margaret had a point.

Gloria finished her bag of chips, crumpled the empty wrapper and tossed it in the nearby trashcan. She wiped her hands on the napkin and reached for her cell phone.

Lucy didn't answer and Gloria left a message for her to call.

"I'm back." Gloria whirled around to find Andrea standing in the doorway.

Andrea was holding three bags of food in her hand. "I thought you all might be hungry."

Gloria groaned.

Margaret patted her stomach. "I'm starving." She winked at Gloria and reached for one of the bags.

Gloria thought Margaret was just being nice until she noticed that Margaret finished eating the entire second sandwich. "Now, I'm full," she declared.

Andrea plopped into the empty seat on the other side of Margaret's bed. She turned to the woman in the bed. "What did the doctors say?"

"That I'm too crotchety to be going anywhere anytime soon," she joked. "Seriously, I have a mild concussion but they decided to torture me by making me stay overnight."

Andrea turned to Gloria for confirmation.

Gloria nodded. "It's true. All of it except for the crotchety part."

Gloria unwrapped the turkey wrap Andrea had given her. "Thanks for the sandwich, Andrea. That was very thoughtful." She lifted the wrap to her mouth and took a big bite. "Do you have any plans later?"

Andrea shook her head. "Nope. I dropped Alice off at the Acosta's farm earlier this morning so I'm on my own until later this evening when I have to run by there to pick her up. Why?"

"I was thinking about attending a candlelight vigil they're having this evening for Bill."

Andrea arched a brow. "The killer always returns to the scene of the crime…or goes to the victim's memorial or funeral."

"It's worth a shot," Gloria said. "Don is coming back around six so we can go right from here to the park." She glanced down at her outfit. She was wearing her standard spy gear from when the girls had gone to Bill's house earlier, which consisted of a black turtleneck, black slacks and dark brown flats.

Andrea always looked nice. She was wearing a pink cashmere sweater and black slacks. They would definitely pass muster for grieving attire.

Lucy returned Gloria's call a couple hours later and when Gloria explained that Andrea and she wanted to attend Bill's vigil, Lucy paused.

"You don't have to go," Gloria told her.

"I'm torn," Lucy admitted. "On the one hand I want to pay my respects." There was silence on the other end. "Do you think it will look odd if I don't at least make an appearance?"

Gloria picked at a piece of lint on her pants. "Like an admission of guilt? Maybe." She wasn't sure if it would look suspicious if Lucy went or if Lucy didn't go.

"I can meet you there," Lucy said in a small voice. "What time?"

Gloria glanced at her watch. "How does 6:30 sound? The candlelight vigil starts at 7:00. They're holding it in Besterman Park." Besterman Park was one of the larger parks in Green Springs. In the summertime, the city held concerts, Saturday night movies under the stars and other fun family events in the park.

The girls agreed to meet in the parking lot at 6:30 on the dot.

Andrea and Gloria stepped out of Margaret's room when the doctor stopped by to check on her.

He shut the door for privacy and the girls headed to a small visitors area at the end of the hall.

"Do you think Margaret will be all right?" Andrea fretted.

Gloria patted her hand. "She'll be fine, dear. Like she said, she's too cranky to go anywhere."

She glanced at Andrea's hand. Andrea was wearing a silver band with a row of sapphires on her third finger.

Gloria touched the top of the ring. "That's a beautiful ring, Andrea. Where did you get it?"

Andrea twisted the band between her thumb and forefinger. "Brian surprised me with it a few months back. At first, when he handed me the box, I thought it was an engagement ring," she admitted.

Gloria could not help herself. "Were you disappointed that it wasn't?"

Andrea lifted her hand and gazed at the band. "Yes and no. I mean, Brian and I have talked about settling down." She wrinkled her nose. "It's just that we both have homes that we love and both of us are too stubborn to move in with the other."

"Kind of silly, huh," Andrea added.

"No. That's not silly at all." Gloria and Paul had run into the same complication. Both of them had farms that had been in their respective families for decades. Farms that they hoped to pass on to the next generation.

In Gloria's case, her two sons weren't at all interested in farming or the farmhouse.

Gloria's oldest son, Eddie, lived in Chicago with his wife, Karen. Her middle child, Ben, lived in Houston, Texas with his wife Kelly and their twins. That left Jill, Gloria's youngest child. Jill wasn't interested in living on the farm.

Jill's two young sons, Gloria's grandsons, Tyler and Ryan were a different story. She would bet money the two of them would fight over the farm. Just the thought of her two beloved grandsons made her smile.

"Do what Paul and I are going to do," she suggested. "Share time between both. Eventually, the living arrangements will work themselves out." At least Gloria hoped they would.

It reminded her that Paul's son, Jeff, and Jeff's wife, Tina, had recently moved back in with him. Maybe it wouldn't be an issue for them, after all.

Andrea sighed. "Yeah, you're right. Maybe we're putting too much emphasis on material things."

Gloria quoted a favorite Bible verse:

"Do not lay up for yourselves treasures on earth, where moth and rust destroy and where thieves break in and steal, but lay up for yourselves treasures in heaven, where neither moth nor rust destroys and where thieves do not break in and steal. For where your treasure is, there your heart will be also." Matthew 6:19-21 ESV

Andrea closed her eyes and nodded. "Yeah. I need to remember that. Life is so temporal."

Gloria thought about Andrea's first husband, Daniel Malone, who had been murdered.

Andrea tugged on a strand of blonde hair. "Every time I think about Daniel and how important material possessions were to him, I try to remind myself that I don't want to end up like that."

Andrea impulsively reached over and hugged Gloria. "That's what I love about you. You have a way of putting everything into perspective without even trying."

Gloria hugged her back. "I believe that it is God speaking through me, that's all."

Andrea looked over Gloria's shoulder. "The doctor just came out of Margaret's room. Time to find out what he has to say."

Chapter 15

They quietly made their way over to the doctor, who was standing outside Margaret's door scribbling notes inside a chart.

"Hello..." Gloria paused. She nodded toward Margaret's room. "How is she?"

The doctor looked up. "She appears to be doing much better now but we'll still keep her overnight for observation. I'll check on her one final time before my shift ends."

He went on. "Doctor Gillivray will be here later to check on her."

Andrea and Gloria would be long gone by then. At least Don would be here to keep Margaret company.

Gloria thanked the doctor for the update and the girls stepped back into the room. Margaret, who held the TV remote in her hand, glanced up. "The TV shows here leave much to be desired."

Margaret loved to say that idle hands were the devil's tools and she rarely watched TV. She was a movie, buff, though, and loved to watch movies in the theater room Don and she had built in their basement.

Every once in a blue moon, when a hot new release came out, they hosted a movie night and would invite a bunch of friends over to watch it. The guests would play board games and munch on finger foods. Afterwards they would settle in with huge bowls of popcorn and soft drinks to watch the movie.

She jabbed the "off" button and tossed the remote on the end of the bed. "Nothing but a bunch of junk."

"Have Don bring your e-reader," Gloria suggested.

Margaret snapped her fingers. "Great idea. Why didn't I think of that?"

The girls settled in again to wait for Don and the rest of the afternoon flew by.

"There's my girl," Don's loud voice boomed from the doorway.

He was carrying a large bouquet of zinnias, marigolds and sunflowers. There were even a few crimson-colored roses tucked into the arrangement.

Margaret's eyes lit up when she saw her husband and noticed the bouquet. "For me?" she gushed.

Don set the arrangement on the table and bent down to kiss his wife.

Gloria and Andrea silently slipped out of the room.

Gloria gave Don a quick wave as they made a hasty exit.

Margaret was in safe hands now and Gloria was thrilled that Don had been thoughtful enough to bring his bride flowers.

Gloria nodded to the nurses as they passed the nurses station and stepped over to the bank of elevators on the other side.

When they reached the main level, Andrea led the way to her truck, parked in the visitor parking lot.

Andrea had not taken the time to wash the mud off her truck. It was still covered with a thick coat of caked mud. She hopped into the driver's seat. "Do you mind if I stop by the car wash and rinse some of this mud off?"

Gloria reached for her seatbelt. "Not at all dear. Be my guest."

Andrea drove to the nearest car wash and ran her truck through twice.

When they finished washing the truck, they turned onto the main road and headed toward the park, which was on the edge of the downtown area.

The parking lot was packed. Andrea drove around several times before she was able to find an open spot.

Lucy wandered over as Andrea and Gloria climbed out of the truck. She tugged on the edge of her jacket sleeve and cast a wary eye toward the clusters of people who started to gather near the fountain, located in the center of the park. "I'm nervous," she admitted.

Gloria wrapped an arm around her shoulder. "We're right here with you. Don't worry. We don't have to stay long." Just long enough to study the mourners.

The trio walked across the parking lot and through the wrought iron gate entrance.

"Can you believe how many people are here?" Lucy whispered. "I didn't know that Bill even knew this many people."

They had just entered the park when Andrea came to an abrupt halt. "That's it!"

"What's it?" Lucy asked.

Andrea pointed to a beat up, rusted out, red car outside the gate. "That is the car that ran me off the road!"

***

The girls hurried out of the park and made their way over to the jalopy.

Gloria peered inside the driver's side window. "Are you sure?"

"Positive!" Andrea walked around the back and studied the bumper. "I remember this sticker." She lifted her foot and kicked the back of the car with the heel of her shoe. "Piece of crap!"

Her eyes blazed as she gazed through the gates of the park. "Whoever tried to run me off the road is inside."

Andrea marched through the gates as she made her way over to the fountain. She had no idea who she was looking for but she vaguely remembered the vehicle had one lone occupant and that person was wearing a dark hat or had dark hair. That left the field wide open.

Gloria cupped her hands together and pressed them against Andrea's ear. "You'd be better off watching the vehicle to see who gets into it," she whispered.

"Right!" Andrea nodded. "I'll be out on the sidewalk if you need me."

She turned on her heel and stomped out of the park. Gloria shook her head. "I don't believe I have ever seen Andrea so fired up," she said.

Lucy had to agree. "Me either." She turned her attention to the crowd of people. "We don't have candles."

Lucy had a point. They didn't have candles. She glanced around. Others were "candleless," as well.

Lucy's eyes darted back and forth, as she studied the growing crowd. "I have cold feet."

"You can do this." Gloria propelled her forward and they joined the outer fringe of mourners.

"I think I'm going to throw up," Lucy groaned.

"Do you want to take a walk?" Gloria wasn't sure if that would help. It certainly couldn't hurt.

"No."

Gloria glanced at Lucy's face, which was pale and pinched. Maybe this hadn't been such a great idea, after all. "We can leave if you want."

"No. It's too late. We're already here."

"Focus your attention on possible suspects," Gloria suggested. "That will take your mind off the other."

Lucy nodded. "Good idea." She studied the faces. Lucy recognized several people. Some of them were Bill's hunting and fishing pals. Bill's daughters and their spouses stood close to the fountain.

The employees from All Seasons Sporting Goods gathered in a small cluster near Bill's family.

"Over there…near the angel statue," Lucy pointed.

Gloria's eyes drifted to the angel.

"The lady with the hoochie mama outfit. That's Bill's ex-wife, Victoria."

Lucy had given an accurate description of Bill's ex. She was wearing a tight fitting, hip hugging, super short black dress that showed too much cleavage, at least in Gloria's opinion. "Where does she live?"

"Detroit, I think."

Detroit. The same place where the gun shop was located. Gloria wondered if there was a possible connection. Was Bill's ex-wife somehow involved in his death? Had she hired a hitman?

Surely, Bill had a will and that would be the first place investigators would look.

The girls wove their way through the throng of people and studied the faces as they worked their way around the cement fountain. Hundreds of lit candles lined the ledge.

The glow from the candles bounced off the tranquil water that surrounded the fountain. It was peaceful and serene.

Someone began to sing, "Amazing Grace." Gloria and Lucy joined in. A tear rolled down Lucy's cheek and she hastily brushed it away.

"You!" A woman's shrill voice cut through the solemn reverence of the song.

All eyes turned as Victoria Volk marched across the grass and stopped in front of Lucy. She lifted a blood red fingernail and pointed it at Lucy. "What are *you* doing here?" she shrieked.

"I'm paying my respects," Lucy answered in a calm even voice.

"Out!" Victoria shouted, her fists clenched at her sides. "Get out!"

The crowd parted and Lucy and Gloria shuffled to the park's entrance. Every eye was on the two of them as they made their way down the sidewalk and through the gates.

Gloria opened her mouth to speak but was interrupted by the sound of tires squealing. She looked up just in time to see a car swerve off to one side. It almost sideswiped another car before it careened out of the parking lot and onto the road.

She could hear the roar of the car's engine as it raced off into the dark night.

"I know who you are!" A voice screamed. The voice, a woman's voice, sounded very familiar. It was Andrea. She was standing near the center of the parking lot, shaking her fist in the direction of the car.

"Looks like Andrea found the car's owner," Gloria commented.

Andrea stomped over to the spot that the car in question had just vacated. She nearly collided with Lucy and Gloria. "Oh! There you are!"

She waved her arms wildly in the air. "I know who ran me off the road."

"Who was it?" Gloria asked.

"That kid. The one that works at All Seasons Sporting Goods…Zeke something."

Chapter 16

Gloria was stunned. "Zeke?" Why would Zeke try to run Andrea and Margaret off the road?

Andrea's chest heaved as she tried to catch her breath. "Yeah! When I confronted him, he shoved me to the ground, hopped in his piece of crap car and drove off. He knew he ran me into the ditch!"

Gloria shifted her feet and stared at the exit. At the very least, Zeke was a terrible driver and inconsiderate to boot. Maybe there was more to the story. Gloria remembered how he had said that Bill told him to keep an eye on the other employees. That someone was stealing money.

Bill's key to the gun case was missing...or was it? What if Zeke was staying in Bill's house? Maybe he was in cahoots with Maxim, the gun dealer?

There were still Randy and Barbara. Gloria wasn't ruling anyone out.

She turned to Andrea. "Do you have time to swing by All Seasons?"

Andrea reached for her keys. "Absolutely. I want to punch that little punk's lights out."

Gloria smiled. The visual of tiny little Andrea punching anyone was hilarious. The girl had spunk. Gloria had to give her that.

"I'll ride with you," Lucy offered. "We can stop back by here and pick up my jeep on the way home."

The girls piled into Andrea's truck and maneuvered out of the packed parking lot. When they reached the road, Gloria turned to Andrea. "If we track him down, under no circumstances are you to approach him. He may have a weapon."

Andrea tightened her jaw. "I know. I'm just so dang mad." She pounded the steering wheel in frustration. "That moron hurt Margaret."

Gloria shook her head. Zeke had seemed like a nice kid. Maybe she had him all wrong.

Andrea pulled the truck into the dark, deserted parking lot of the store and drove around back. The lot was empty. There was no sign of a rusted out two-door car. Gloria was relieved. A confrontation this late at night behind a deserted building was a bad idea.

She knew Andrea carried a concealed weapon. Not that she believed Andrea would use it unless she absolutely had to. Of course, if this young man was a killer, then maybe they would need it.

"We should head back," Gloria suggested. It had been a very long day and she was exhausted. So much had happened in such a short amount of time, she wasn't sure if she was coming or going.

"Do you think this Zeke guy is living at Bill's place?" Lucy asked.

Gloria had had the same thought. It was quite possible. "Maybe."

Lucy turned to Gloria, her expression anxious. "It wouldn't take long to take a quick run by there to check it out."

"I'm game," Andrea blurted out. More than anything, she wanted to confront this character, to demand an explanation for purposely driving her into the ditch.

Gloria stared out the front windshield. If Zeke thought they were onto him, he might bolt. They may never catch Bill's killer.

If he was the killer, and he knew they were onto him, would he lie in wait, expecting them to show up? She wasn't keen on walking blindly into a dangerous situation.

Maybe he was just a dumb kid who did a dumb thing and then got caught. Maybe not.

Andrea patted her purse. "I'm packing heat."

Gloria groaned. "That's what I was afraid of."

Lucy directed Andrea to Bill's street and then pointed to the long, winding drive that led to his house.

Andrea slowed the truck. "Should we or shouldn't we?" She didn't wait for an answer as she cranked the wheel and started down the narrow drive.

"Kill the lights," Lucy suggested.

Andrea promptly shut off the headlamps but left the fog lights on.

The closer they got, the louder Gloria's heart pounded in her chest. Were they driving right into a trap?

Technically, they were trespassing. If there were someone living in Bill's house with his permission, that person would have every right to call the cops.

Gloria decided to keep that thought to herself.

When they reached the end of the drive, the ranch house came into view.

Curtains covered the large front picture window. Small rays of light beamed out from the edges. "Someone is in there," Lucy said.

Andrea let off the gas and the truck coasted the rest of the way. Parked next to the house was a vehicle, but it wasn't Zeke's rust bucket. It was a newer sedan and one that Gloria didn't recognize.

"I wonder who that belongs to," Gloria said. She reached inside her purse and pulled out her cell phone. She switched the phone to on and handed it to Lucy, who was in the passenger seat. "Take a picture of the license plate."

Lucy reached for the phone. "We're not close enough."

"That can be arranged." Andrea tapped the gas pedal and the truck lurched forward. When they got close, Lucy lifted the phone and snapped a photo. "I hope it turns out. It's awfully dark."

"Four TX E71," Gloria repeated the numbers in her head. "Text that to me."

Lucy handed the phone back. "I have no idea how to operate your phone."

She reached in her pocket, pulled out her own phone and began tapping the screen. "Done."

"Uh-oh," Andrea moaned. "Someone is coming!"

"Burn rubber lady!" Gloria shouted.

Andrea obeyed Gloria's instructions, literally, as she jammed the truck into reverse, skidded to a halt, shoved it into drive and stomped on the gas pedal.

The truck sailed along the drive at a good clip and even went airborne a couple times, as the truck zoomed over several ruts in the drive.

"Someone should fix that drive," Gloria said. She glanced behind her. There were two lights. Headlights. "I think they're following us."

Andrea squealed out of the drive and careened onto the street. She pressed her foot down on the gas and the truck roared off down the road. Gloria was glad she wasn't driving. She didn't do too well driving after dark.

Andrea had no problem at all.

Gloria tugged on the edge of her seatbelt to make sure it was securely fastened. She glanced behind her.

Off in the distance was a set of dim lights. She wasn't certain if it was the same vehicle from Bill's place or perhaps someone else.

When they reached Green Springs' city limits, Andrea slowed. "Now what?"

"I need to pick up my jeep," Lucy reminded her.

"Right." Andrea turned onto the main road and pulled into the park. The lot was still half-full and Lucy's jeep was parked in the back.

Andrea stopped in front of Lucy's jeep. Lucy opened the door and started to climb out.

"We'll follow you home," Andrea offered.

"She's not going anywhere," Gloria stated.

"Huh?" Lucy frowned.

Gloria pointed at the jeep. "Your tires. They're flat."

Sure enough, all four of Lucy's tires were flatter than pancakes. "Victoria Volk," Lucy fumed. "I'll bet money that woman flattened my tires."

"Hopefully she just let the air out of them." Gloria saw dollar signs at the thought of Lucy having to buy four brand new tires.

"I have a flashlight." Lucy stepped over to her passenger side door and pulled it open. She reached into her glove box and pulled out a flashlight.

Andrea and Gloria climbed out of the truck. The girls inspected all four tires and were relieved that they hadn't been slashed.

Andrea shuffled over to her truck, leaned against the front quarter panel and crossed her arms. "Now what?"

Lucy frowned. "No repair shop for miles around is open this late."

"What about Gus?" Andrea asked. He had been a lifesaver earlier when Andrea had been in the ditch.

"Smart thinking." Gloria pulled her phone from her purse, switched it to "on," scrolled through the screen and tapped Gus' cell phone number.

Lucy prayed he would be able to help.

"Hi Gus. It's me Gloria. We have a little emergency," she said.

She went on. "We're down here at Besterman Park. Someone let the air out of Lucy's tires." She paused. "Uh-huh. Yep. Okay we'll be here."

Lucy grabbed the phone from Gloria's hand. "Gus. You're a lifesaver. I love you. If Mary Beth ever leaves you, I want to marry you! Okay. Bye."

She handed the phone back. "He said he'll be here in less than half an hour."

Gus, the sweetheart, arrived right on time. He was driving a tow truck but it wasn't the same one that he had used earlier to pull Andrea's truck out of the ditch. This wrecker had a flat bed.

He slid out of the driver's seat and made his way over to where the girls were waiting. He nodded at Gloria and glanced at Andrea. "You again."

Andrea blushed. "Yeah. I'm having quite a day," she admitted.

He turned his attention to the jeep. "What'cha got?"

"Someone let the air out of my tires," Lucy explained.

Gus walked over to the jeep. He inspected the tires.

Lucy hovered nearby.

Gus shook his head and rose to his feet. "There's no way to air them here. I'll have to load 'er on the back and take her back to the station to air them up."

He lowered the flatbed of the truck and then hooked a hook, connected to a towrope to the front of the jeep. Next, he pulled the jeep onto the bed and secured all four tires with tire chains. He tugged on each of the tire chains to make sure the car was secure and then leveled the platform. They were ready to roll.

Lucy rode with Gus while Gloria and Andrea followed behind.

When they got to Gus's shop, he wasted no time airing her tires. Gus told her he was only going charge her $50 but Lucy insisted it was more.

Gus held up both hands. "Nah! You know I can't charge you more, Lucy. After all, you proposed to me," he joked.

He wouldn't take another dime so Lucy paid the $50.

One the way out, Gloria slipped another $50 in his jacket pocket.

Gus shook his head and reached for the money. "Gloria..."

Gloria put a hand on his arm. "Gus, you're a sweetheart...salt of the earth. You deserve it."

Gus clamped his mouth shut and then grinned. "Thanks Gloria."

The long day and chain of events had taken their toll and the girls were exhausted.

Andrea yawned and lifted her hands over her head. "I better get going. I still have to pick up Alice."

Gloria hugged Andrea and patted her back. "Be careful." She crawled into Lucy's passenger seat and placed her head on the headrest. "I'm exhausted."

"Me, too," Lucy agreed.

Thankfully, they weren't far from home.

Lucy pulled the jeep into Gloria's drive and circled around until the passenger door faced the side porch. "Talk to you in the morning."

"You got it." Gloria unfastened her seatbelt and opened the door.

She slipped out of the passenger seat. "Be careful going home."

Lucy rubbed her eyes. "I will."

Gloria closed the passenger door and slowly walked up the porch steps.

She could see Mally's face peeking out through the lower glass pane. Poor Mally had been home alone for most of the day. A wave of guilt washed over Gloria.

Lucy waited until Gloria was safely inside before she pulled out of the drive.

Inside the kitchen, Gloria peeked out the kitchen window and watched as Lucy turned onto the road.

As soon as Lucy's jeep turned onto the road, a vehicle appeared out of nowhere and began to tailgate Lucy. From the mercury light on the far side of the barn, Gloria caught a glimpse of the vehicle as it zoomed by.

Her blood froze. Gloria recognized the vehicle!

Chapter 17

Gloria, keys still in her hand, yanked the porch door open and raced down the steps. Lucy was in trouble. She could feel it in her bones.

All this time Gloria had been foolish to think that someone's main objective was to frame Lucy. Not only did they want to frame Lucy, they wanted her gone. As in six-foot-under gone.

Her mind raced. She did the only thing she could think to do as she slammed Annabelle in reverse and barreled out of the driveway.

With one eye on the road and the other on her phone, Gloria dialed Paul's cell phone and prayed he would pick up.

"Hello?"

"Lucy is in trouble," she blurted out. "She just dropped me off at home and when she pulled out of the drive, a vehicle raced up behind and began tailgating her."

"Did you recognize the vehicle?"

"I did," Gloria said. She told Paul who owned the vehicle and gave him the make and color.

"Where are you going now?" Paul, who had stopped by the Montbay County Sheriff station to drop off some paperwork, headed for the door.

"To Lucy's house." Gloria glanced in the rearview mirror. "Whoever it is - is out to harm her. I feel it in my bones."

"Don't do anything, rash, Gloria."

"I-I'll do whatever I can to save Lucy," Gloria replied. She wouldn't make a promise that she couldn't keep.

Gloria disconnected the line and dropped the phone in her lap. When Lucy's place was in sight, she eased her foot off the gas and slowed the car. It was too dark to see!

Gloria drove to the corner, turned around and did another drive by. Lucy's jeep was parked close to the house.

Directly behind Lucy's jeep was Bill's truck. Someone, most likely the killer, had the nerve to move into Bill's house. Not only that, they had somehow managed to steal his truck!

She remembered the backpack sitting next to the bed. Then she remembered Zeke, who had run Andrea off the road. Maybe Zeke was trying to kill them all!

Gloria began to feel lightheaded and her pulse raced. Now was not the time to feel faint!

She gripped the steering wheel tightly. "Think, Gloria, think," she whispered aloud.

She pressed on the gas pedal and drove past. At the next corner, she turned onto the side road and glanced down at the clock on the dashboard.

Paul was at least 20 minutes out…Lucy might not have 20 minutes!

Gloria studied both sides of the dirt road in search of a place to pull off. When she found an even spot where the tall grass had been trampled, she pulled off the road.

Gloria fumbled with her cell phone as she dialed Lucy's number. She prayed her friend would answer, and that everything would be all right but it went right to voice mail. She didn't dare try the house phone.

She put the car in park, killed the lights and switched the engine off. She shoved her purse on the floor and eased out of the driver's seat.

The weeds pressed against the side of the car and she batted them away as she eased the driver's side door shut.

The quarter moon, along with what seemed like a million stars, gave off a little light. Other than that, the country road was pitch black.

Gloria shoved her cell phone in her back pocket and waited for a moment to give her eyes a chance to adjust to the lack of light.

She was too far away to see Lucy's house, hidden by a row of tall trees that lined the edge of the farm field.

Gloria studied the edge of the field. She had two choices: either she could take to the field and chance stumbling on a rock and injuring herself, which wouldn't help Lucy at all, or she could walk along the edge of the road.

She opted for the path of least resistance...the road.

"Please God. Protect Lucy," she whispered. "And me," she added.

Gloria jogged down the road as fast as she dared. When she reached the corner, she made a sharp right and headed to the house.

She could see the corner of Lucy's house now and she slowed her pace, just a little. Gloria knew the layout of Lucy's place almost as well as her own.

She tiptoed to the edge of the yard and prayed that Jasper, Lucy's dog, wouldn't spot her and start barking.

She let out a sigh of relief that the front of the house was dark.

Gloria snaked around the back of the house and darted to the shed...Lucy's weapons shed. Gloria knew that the shed was loaded with guns. Gloria just needed one.

When she got to the edge of the shed, she dropped to her knees and turned to face the kitchen window.

Lucy passed in front of the window. Gloria narrowed her eyes and studied the pinched expression on her face.

Lucy turned to face whoever was in the kitchen with her and her lips moved. She shook her head violently.

Gloria's blood grew cold. If she had to guess, Lucy was pleading for her life!

With renewed determination, Gloria hustled around the side of the shed and over to the entrance door. She grabbed the handle and turned the knob. The door was locked!

She rattled the handle in desperation and prayed that somehow God would unlock the door for her.

Frustration spilled over and Gloria whacked her open palm on the door.

"Dummy!" she scolded herself...nothing like drawing attention to herself.

She crept to the back corner of the shed and began to pace. "I need to find a way into that shed!"

Gloria remembered not long ago that Max, Lucy's boyfriend, had accidentally shot out one of the shed windows. Lucy had boarded it up and was now waiting for repair people to install a special order piece of glass.

Gloria retraced her steps and made her way over to the boarded up window. With both hands, she pressed against the thin piece of paneling that covered the opening. It bowed under the pressure. She pushed harder and it gave a little more.

Gloria closed her eyes, offered up a prayer and pushed with all of her strength.

Pop!

The flimsy piece of material popped out and clattered on the cement floor inside the shed. Gloria frowned at the square window frame and then looked down at her body. It would be a tight fit but she had to try!

Gloria placed both hands on the windowsill and pulled herself up onto the frame. Her feet dangled in the air while her head tottered back and forth inside. *I really need to hit the gym.*

Finally, gravity took over and Gloria landed on the cement floor of the shed with a loud thud. Her knee cracked. She gingerly rubbed her kneecap and hoped the noise was a joint and not a bone.

She scrambled to her feet and limped to the other side of the room. The only light was the light from the window she had just come through.

"Handguns, Gloria. Where does Lucy keep her handguns?" She forced herself to focus on the task at hand, as she reached for the large upper cabinet. Although there was a lock, it wasn't latched.

She quickly slipped the lock from the door latch bracket and set it on the workbench. She opened the cabinet door and peered inside. It was too dark to see anything.

Gloria stuck her hand inside the cabinet and felt around. The shelf was full of guns! How was Gloria to know which one would work best? The only gun she'd ever handled was the one small handgun she had at home. Lucy's guns seemed a whole lot bigger!

She didn't have time to decide which gun would work best. Any gun that would fire would have to be good enough. She reached for the nearest gun, ejected the clip and checked for bullets. The gun was loaded.

She snapped the base back in place, shoved the gun in the waistband of her pants and glanced around. There was no way was she going to crawl back out the window. Instead, she unlocked the shed door and slipped outside.

Gloria inched along the side of the shed and around to the back. She lowered down and tiptoed across the open yard until she reached the edge of the house. She dropped to her knees and crawled along the white lattice that covered the bottom of the porch.

When she reached the other side, she slithered to a standing position and peeked in the corner of the window.

Lucy was still standing near the window, her face pale and her lips drawn in a tight line.

Gloria's eyes widened when the barrel of a gun came into view. The gun was pointed right at Lucy! A tall shadow flitted back and forth but Gloria couldn't see who it was.

There was no way Gloria could sneak in, not with the killer guarding the door.

Gloria bit her lower lip. In the back of the house was a set of steps that led to the basement. It was Gloria's only hope!

She crept along the side and then the front of the house until she reached the steps. Gloria leaned against the side of the house and plucked her cell phone from her back pocket.

She turned her cell phone on and it gave off just enough light for Gloria to creep down the steps to the basement door.

Gloria had been nagging Lucy for months to get the basement door fixed. The door lock was broken and if you wiggled the knob just right, the lock would pop. She prayed that Lucy hadn't gotten around to fixing it yet.

Gloria grasped the handle and jiggled it back and forth. She prayed that Lucy and whoever was upstairs wouldn't hear.

Woof! Woof! Off in the distance, Gloria heard a dog bark. It was Jasper! Lucy's dog, Jasper, had heard her!

Desperate to get inside, Gloria frantically twisted the handle and finally, it popped. She turned the knob and slowly pushed the door open.

The mixture of garlic and mothballs assaulted Gloria's nose. Lucy had had a problem with mice a short time ago and read online that if she combined the two smells, it would drive out any rodent. Or vampires.

She waved her hand across her face. Gloria took a step across the threshold when something dark and moving at the speed of light crashed into the side of her leg almost knocking her over. It was Jasper. Lucy had let him outside. He wagged his tail and nudged Gloria.

Gloria knelt down and patted his head. "Good doggie, Jasper. Don't bark at Auntie Gloria," she warned.

Jasper licked the side of her face and then darted back out into the dark yard.

Gloria let out a sigh of relief, stepped inside the basement and quietly closed the door behind her.

Lucy's basement was crammed from floor to ceiling with boxes and discarded furniture. Storage shelves lined an entire wall. On those shelves were tidy rows of canned goods.

Centered between two shelves was the door leading to the upstairs. The door was ajar.

Gloria stepped over to the door and gently pushed. She slipped through the crack in the door and pressed her body against the wall.

She pulled the gun from her waistband and put one foot on the bottom stair tread. "Dear God, protect us!"

Chapter 18

Gloria dropped down on all fours and crept up the steps. The safety was still on the gun and she was careful to keep the trigger away from her trembling fingers.

The old shag carpet, threadbare in spots caused Gloria's knees to ache. Or maybe it was the tumble she had taken while breaking into the shed.

A sharp nail jutted up from one of the steps and stabbed her thumb.

Gloria lifted the wounded digit for a quick inspection. A small trace of blood appeared and she wondered how long it had been since her last tetanus shot. She briefly decided that if she couldn't remember, it was probably time for a booster.

This would only matter if Lucy - and she - made it out alive.

She had a fleeting thought that Paul should only be minutes away. Would Paul come in, guns blazing? Would he decide to surround the place and the girls would end up in a hostage situation? She hoped not.

Gloria was halfway to the top when she heard the sound of voices as they drifted down the basement steps.

It was Lucy's voice and a male voice. The two of them were arguing.

As Gloria neared the top, she realized she recognized the deep voice. It was a voice from beyond the grave!

At the top of the stairs, Gloria eased along the far wall as she made her way through the pantry and peeked around the edge of the door and into the kitchen.

Bill's back was to Gloria as he faced Lucy, his gun pointed at her chest. "There's no point in discussing this any further, Lucy. I already have blood on my hands. The FTA was hot on my trail. The only loose end right now is you."

Bill's hollow laughter filled the room and sent a shiver down Gloria's spine. "Now that you've written your suicide note, explaining that you killed yourself because you were so distraught over my death, the only thing left is for you to finish the job."

Bill pulled a handkerchief from his front pocket and wrapped it around the metal grip. He lifted the gun and pointed it at Lucy's head.

At that precise moment, Gloria launched her body at Bill.

Bill lost his balance and stumbled forward.

Lucy lunged at him as she reached for the gun, which fired into the air.

Bill staggered to the side, the gun still tightly gripped in his hand.

Lucy dove for his knees.

Gloria lifted her own gun and flipped the safety lever. She pressed the barrel against his temple.

"Freeze!"

"Drop the gun!" she shouted. "Drop the gun or I'll shoot you dead! I swear I'll do it!"

Bill dropped the gun and it clattered to the floor.

Lucy dove for the gun.

Bill kicked it away and at the same time, kicked Lucy in the head.

For a brief second, Gloria shifted her attention to Lucy.

Bill, seeing that Gloria was distracted, seized his opportunity to overpower Gloria and swiped at the gun in her hand.

The two of them struggled for the weapon. Bill was bigger and stronger than Gloria and although she fought with all that she had, she was no match.

Gloria's grip loosened, and Bill started to get the upper hand when the kitchen door burst open and Paul plowed in. "Freeze!"

Bill let go of the gun.

Gloria quickly stumbled backward and fell to the floor.

Lucy lay on the floor, curled up in a ball, her head in her hands. When she pulled her hands away, Gloria could see a large smear of blood near her temple.

Two uniformed officers stormed into the kitchen and quickly handcuffed a very-much-alive Bill Volk.

Gloria crawled over to her friend. "Lucy! Lucy, are you okay?"

The crimson blood was a stark contrast to Lucy's ghostly white complexion. "I-I think so."

The two crawled over to the cabinets and leaned against them as the shock of what had just happened began to sink in.

The two officers led Bill Volk out of the house. Paul followed behind.

It was several long moments before Paul appeared back inside the kitchen. "You could've been killed," Paul said.

"Lucy was almost a goner," Gloria argued. "A few more seconds and she would have been dead. Bill was cleaning his prints off the gun when I surprised him."

Paul bent down to examine Lucy's injury. "Do you want me to call an ambulance?"

Lucy slowly shook her head. "Nah. My noggin is thicker than that."

"I'm just glad it's finally over," she added.

"Me too." Gloria couldn't agree more.

The girls slowly rose to their feet and made their way over to the kitchen table. It was still hard to believe that Bill was alive...and a killer. A killer who had staged his own death.

The police questioned Lucy at length and then asked Gloria several questions. After they left, Paul stayed behind. "You'll need to come by the station tomorrow to fill out some paperwork."

Lucy nodded. "I'll be there."

"I'll be with you," Gloria reassured her friend.

Paul stayed long enough to check the entire house and grounds to make sure there wasn't another person hiding out, waiting in the wings to finish the job.

When he finished his search, Gloria walked Paul out to his patrol car. "Thank you for saving my...saving our lives."

Paul pulled Gloria close and set his chin on top of her head. "Why can't you take up something safe like origami or stamp collecting," he groaned.

"Or pottery," she reminded him.

Despite the gravity of the situation, Gloria giggled. "Maybe I'll take up martial arts instead."

Paul snorted. "Well, that would at least be useful."

He kissed her tenderly and then made her promise to give him a call when she was safe and sound at home.

Jasper had wandered back in the kitchen and looked up at Gloria when she stepped inside. She reached down and hugged his neck. "Good dog. You didn't even bark at me."

"He didn't?" Lucy turned to Jasper. "What kind of watch dog are you?"

"The best," Gloria said.

Lucy fixed a pot of tea while Gloria hovered over her. After what had happened to Margaret earlier, she wanted to make sure her friend was all right before she left.

"Bill told me that he was in trouble with the law so he staged his own death. I asked him whose body was discovered in the house across from yours and he mumbled something about a traitor." Lucy shuddered.

"He went into great detail on how he had used a gun, just like mine, to kill the guy and then disfigured his face so that he couldn't easily be identified." Lucy went on. "In his demented mind, he figured by the time police found out it wasn't his body, he'd be long gone."

Gloria finished her cup of tea. "That is just unbelievable. You think you know someone and then something like this happens."

Gloria's eyes drooped and she began to nod off at the table.

"You should go home," Lucy urged. "It's late."

Gloria nodded. She didn't have an ounce of energy left to fight her. "Can you take me down to get my car? It's in the field next door."

Lucy frowned. "That's right. I forgot all about it." She shook her head as if to rid herself of the cobwebs.

The girls climbed into Lucy's jeep and headed to the next street. Gloria's car was where she had left it and Lucy waited until her friend was safely inside the car before she pulled back onto the road.

Lucy turned off into her drive and Gloria finished the short drive home.

When she got back to the farm, Gloria let Mally out for a short run.

She let her beloved pooch back in the kitchen, shut the door and clicked the lock in place.

Gloria barely had enough strength to brush her teeth. She turned off the bathroom light, stumbled to her bedroom and fell into bed, clothes and all.

Chapter 19

Gloria was out like a light. It was 9:45 a.m. before she heard Mally, who stood in the bedroom doorway and began to whine.

Gloria flung back the covers and reached for her robe. "Okay. I hear you loud and clear."

She let Mally out onto the porch and then made her way to the kitchen counter to start a pot of coffee. She added an extra half scoop of grounds. Today would be another long one and Gloria knew she would need that extra shot of caffeine to make it through.

She had almost finished her first cup of coffee when a movement out of the corner of her eye caught her attention. Five eager faces stared at her through the glass pane of the kitchen door: Dot, Margaret, Lucy, Ruth and last but not least, Andrea.

She clutched her robe around her and shuffled to the door.

"Good morning, sleepy head," Margaret teased.

Gloria reached out and hugged her. "You're out of the hospital."

"I'm fit as a fiddle," Margaret proclaimed. "We've been trying to call you for over an hour now. We decided to call an emergency meeting what with everything that has happened in the last 24 hours."

Gloria swung the door open and motioned them in. "Make yourselves at home. I'll be right back."

She darted into the bedroom, grabbed a pair of blue jeans and purple sweater from the closet and then headed to the bath. She quickly showered, dressed and finger fluffed her hair in place.

Next, she dabbed a little makeup on. Gloria turned to the left, then to the right as she studied her reflection. Despite the lack of sleep and the stress of the last few days, she didn't look too shabby, if she had to say so herself!

The girls had settled in at the table. They were feasting on bagels, muffins and a variety of other baked goodies that Dot had brought with her.

Dot reached for a pecan swirl. "I made another pot of coffee. I hope you don't mind."

"Not at all." Gloria settled into the last empty chair and reached for an "everything" bagel.

Lucy shifted in her seat. "The girls have been dying to know what happened but I told them they would have to wait until you were here to hear the whole story."

Between the two of them, Lucy and Gloria shared the chain of events that had occurred the night before, starting with the moment Gloria caught a glimpse of Bill's truck as it followed Lucy after she pulled out of the drive.

Ruth poured a splash of cream in her coffee. "Did you think it was Bill?"

Gloria drummed her fingers on the tabletop. "No. I thought that whoever had been living in Bill's place had taken his truck."

Lucy shook her head. "All that time, I felt terrible about Bill's death and here he was, faking his own death and then trying to pin it on me."

"When the police didn't arrest you, he got desperate and decided to take you out," Andrea guessed.

"Making it look like a suicide," Dot finished.

Gloria popped the last bite of cream cheese coated bagel in her mouth and wiped her hands on her jeans. "Yep. I can hardly wait to hear what Paul has to say."

Ruth glanced at her watch. "I gotta get back to the post office. If I keep making Kenny hold down the fort, he's gonna want a raise."

Andrea stood, too. "Yeah. I need to go. Alice is chomping at the bit to get over to the puppies."

The rest of the girls headed for the door.

Gloria held it open and followed them out. "How is that going?"

Andrea pulled her keys from her purse. "Great! Thanks to your generous donation, the place is shaping up. You wouldn't even recognize it."

She went on. "A trainer is scheduled to come Monday morning to start his first training session."

Andrea squeezed Gloria's hand. "Thanks to you, they can afford the trainer."

"Are they still going to turn it into a boarding kennel?" Gloria thought that made the most sense.

Maximize the use of space and keeping the cash coming in.

Andrea nodded. "Yep. Marco and Alice are working on the website and online ads, too. Alice is turning into quite the website guru."

Andrea pressed a hand to her cheek. "Oh! And I think there may be a budding romance between Alice and Marco!"

Margaret shook her head. "Well, I'll be darned. Wouldn't that be something?"

Gloria caught a glimpse of Mally out of the corner of her eye. She watched in horror as Mally began watering the edge of one of Andrea's truck tires.

Gloria's hand flew to her mouth. "Oh my gosh, Andrea. I'm so sorry."

Andrea laughed. "That's okay. She probably picked up on Brutus' scent and decided to help him mark his territory."

Dot glanced at her watch. "I should go. Ray is holding down the fort at the restaurant." She reached for the railing.

The word restaurant reminded Gloria of food, which reminded her of Thanksgiving. "Wait! I almost forgot! Thanksgiving. Would any of you be interested in a potluck Thanksgiving here at the farm? I'll make the turkeys and you all bring sides."

The idea was a hit and all agreed they would love to spend the special day with their best friends. Each promised to tell her what they planned to bring by weeks end.

After the last Garden Girl pulled out of the drive, Gloria wandered back inside the house. She had a lot to be thankful for this year, not the least of which was her close-knit group of friends.

Chapter 20

Gloria darted from the oven to the roaster then back to the oven. She hadn't realized that cooking two very large turkeys, along with three pans of stuffing and four large dishes of her made-from-scratch macaroni and cheese would be so much work!

She glanced frantically at the clock on the wall. It was almost time. Almost time for her 20+ guests to start arriving.

The tables had been arranged and her dining room ready for guests. The buffet gleamed from a small spritz of furniture polish and a heavy dose of elbow grease.

The festive fall plates were stacked, the silver polished.

She froze in her tracks when she heard a tap on the backdoor. She thought someone had come early, but it was only her backup troops. Or "troop." It was Paul.

She yanked the door open and dragged him into the kitchen. "Good! You're early." She thrust an apron in his hand. "Put this on."

Paul lifted the apron and stared at the pink pansies that dotted the front. "You have got to be kidding me."

"Fine. Let's switch." Gloria quickly untied her apron, lifted it over her head and handed it to him.

She snatched the one with pretty flowers and dropped it around her neck, quickly tying the back.

Paul wound an arm around her waist. "You need to take a deep breath. Everything will be fine."

Gloria nodded but the wave of panic continued to wash over her. She wasn't sure what had stressed her out so much. After all, it was only friends and family.

Gloria sucked in a breath and forced herself to calm down. "Okay. I'm better now." She gave him a list of chores and then headed to the deep freeze on the front porch in search of corn she had frozen during harvest season.

She had just finished putting her last stick of butter in the butter dish when the guests started to arrive. Soon, the house was brimming with people.

Jill and her family were the last to arrive. Tyler and Ryan raced over to their beloved Grams and wrapped their arms around her waist. "We're starving," they told her.

"I'm hungry enough to eat a whole turkey by myself," Ryan declared.

Gloria swiped a hand across Ryan's blonde locks and planted a kiss on his cheek. "Well, good! At least I won't have to worry about leftovers," she teased.

Each of the Garden Girls arrived laden with goodies for the Thanksgiving feast. There were pots of mashed potatoes, green bean casseroles, sweet, buttery yeast rolls and homemade cranberry sauce.

Dot arrived with every type of dessert conceivable. There was a traditional apple pie, pecan pie, chocolate pie and chocolate cake. Last, but not least, she brought her now famous cream cheese pumpkin pie.

There was so much food, Gloria almost ran out of counter space!

After everyone had arrived, they all assembled in the dining room for a prayer of thanks.

Gloria decided that since Paul would soon be head of the household, it was time to turn over the reins and she asked him to pray.

The room grew silent as the guests bowed their heads in prayer.

"Dear Lord. We are thankful for this day You have given us. Lord, we thank You for each and every one of our family and friends that are here in body and those that are here in spirit. We pray for blessing in each of their lives and ask You to guide us and direct us in the paths You will lead us."

Paul went on. "On this day, we thank You most of all for our Lord and Savior Jesus Christ. In His name we pray amen."

The prayer ended and total chaos ensued.

Gloria stood off to the side and watched as the people who mattered most to her celebrated the day of Thanksgiving.

Gloria loved Christmas. It was her favorite holiday of the year, but Thanksgiving was a close second. It was a time that she could stop and reflect on all of her many blessings.

Paul and Gloria were the last two to fill their plates, and fill them they did. This was the one day of the few days of the year where Gloria gave herself permission to eat anything and everything she wanted.

They settled in to the two empty places near the head of the table. Gloria had managed to fit the children at a card table off to the side while all the adults gathered around two tables she had placed in the shape of a large "L." It was a perfect fit.

Talk of the wedding was the main topic of conversation. When the conversation drifted to Lucy's recent dilemma, everyone quieted down and listened to Paul's explanation of why Bill Volk had faked his own death and tried to frame poor Lucy.

He explained that Bill had recently gotten involved with Artie Maxim, a known criminal who was also a gun salesman. Not only did he sell guns legally, he sold them on the black market, making a tidy profit.

Maxim had somehow convinced Bill that he could make millions by taking in used guns and then reselling them on the streets.

It had worked for several months. Bill had gotten greedy, upping his illegal sales and looking into different avenues to secure more guns. The ATF was onto him and when Bill began to feel the heat, he masterminded his own "murder."

Bill had harbored bitterness towards Lucy for weeks after their break up and he saw the perfect opportunity to frame Lucy, all the while staging his own death.

He had built a secret hideaway underneath his house where he hid out when someone showed up.

Bill had moved into his spare bedroom, where the secret room was located in case the ATF raided the house. He was in the process of buying a home in Mexico and was only days away from leaving the country. Permanently.

Lucy's eyes widened. "So that time we went to his house to snoop around…he was there? Hiding?"

Paul sipped his Coke. "It would seem so."

Gloria reached for a warm roll. "What about the car that ran Andrea off the road? The kid, Zeke, who worked at the store?"

Paul shrugged. "He was just a little thug. He had nothing to do with Bill's scheme. Bill used him to throw suspicion onto Barbara and his brother, Randy."

Gloria turned to Lucy. "We need to do a better job of screening your boyfriends." She winked at Max, Lucy's new boyfriend, who was sitting next to Lucy.

Gloria liked Max. He seemed more "normal" if that made any sense. He wasn't the least perturbed when Lucy shopped or had lunch with friends, unlike Bill who had always insisted that Lucy do what he wanted...mostly hunting, fishing and camping.

Lucy was a tomboy through and through but she still liked to do the girlie stuff.

Jill, Gloria's daughter, reached for the butter. "Did you ever get that deer, Lucy?"

Gloria frowned and gave her daughter a warning look.

It was too late.

Lucy dropped her fork. "Yeah! Hey, Gloria, we only have a few days left for gun season. You want to go tomorrow?"

"Uh..."

Paul reached over and patted Gloria's hand. "Of course she does, Lucy. That's all she can talk about is how much fun she had last time."

Gloria slapped the front of her forehead with the palm of her hand. She vowed that later, after everyone was gone, Paul was going to pay for that comment!

After the last morsel of food that anyone could bear to eat, including the scrumptious desserts Dot had brought, was consumed, the girls made quick work of kitchen clean up while the guys headed to the living room to watch the football game. At least they pretended to watch the game. Every single one of them promptly fell asleep.

Gloria's grandsons darted outside to inspect the tree fort.

Gloria packed the last baggie full of turkey she was sending home and dropped it into Andrea's grocery bag.

"Thanks for the leftovers," Andrea said. "Next is the wedding," she reminded her.

"How's the dress shopping going?" Ruth asked.

Jill snorted. "It's not. I don't believe Mom has even looked for one yet."

"Gloria!" Margaret chided.

Gloria shrugged. "I've been busy," she said. "Besides. I don't want to go alone."

Lucy tapped her on the shoulder. "We'll go with you. How 'bout day after tomorrow?"

Gloria sucked in a deep breath and nodded. Time was running out. The wedding was less than a month away. "Okay."

Alice clapped her hands. "Oooh. This will be so much fun, Miss Gloria."

Margaret dried the last dinner fork and dropped it in the silverware tray. "Great. I have the perfect boutique store in mind. It's in Grand Rapids. We can look for a dress and then have lunch."

Ruth nodded. "Perfect. Even I can go since it's on a Saturday."

Jill headed to the living room. "It's time to round up my troops. We still have to stop by Greg's parents." Jill and her family were the first to leave.

Next was Andrea, Brian and Alice.

Andrea hugged Gloria on her way out the door. "Thanks for the leftovers."

Alice hugged her next. "Everything was delicious, Miss Gloria." She paused. "But if I may suggest, the stuffing...it could use a little more zip." She pinched her fingers together. "Maybe you could add a little jalapeno."

Andrea tugged on her sleeve. "Alice!"

Alice grinned. "It was just a suggestion!"

Lucy and Max were the last to leave. The four of them stood on the porch and chatted. "What do you think will happen to Bill?" Lucy asked.

Paul shifted his tall frame and leaned against the porch post. "He will be gone for a very long time. I doubt he'll live long enough to see the light of day again."

Lucy nodded. She wondered how she could have been such a poor judge of character. "I had no idea."

Paul shoved his hand in his pants pocket. "Don't be so hard on yourself, Lucy. Greed changes people. Greed got the better of him."

"Thanks for saving Gloria and me that night," she said.

Paul grinned at Gloria and winked at Lucy. "She sure does keep me on my toes."

He glanced at Max. "You sure you know what you're getting yourself into?" he joked.

Max shuffled his feet and lifted his head to meet Lucy's eyes. "She's a firecracker, I'll give you that."

Lucy rolled her eyes. "We better get out of here before they decide to take away our car keys," Lucy joked.

Paul and Gloria stood on the steps and watched Lucy and Max drive off in Max's sports car. "He sure does have his hands full," Paul commented.

"Just like you," Gloria teased.

Paul nodded. "Yep. Just like me."

The end.

FREE Books and More!

Visit my website for new releases and special offers: <http://hopecallaghan.com>

If you enjoyed reading "Fall Girl", please take a moment to leave a review. It would be greatly appreciated! Thank you!

The series continues. Look for Garden Girls Book #10, *Home for the Holidays*, December 2015!

Margaret's Magnificent Meatloaf

Ingredients:

1-1/2 lbs. ground beef (I substituted with ground turkey)
1 cup milk
1 egg, slightly beaten
¾ cup soft bread crumbs (I used Club crackers instead)
1/2 medium yellow onion, chopped
1 tbsp. chopped green pepper
4 tbsp. ketchup
1-1/2 tsp salt
1 tsp. sugar (Optional. I think it could be omitted. The sweetness from the Club crackers was enough)

Directions:

-Preheat oven to 350 degrees.
-Combine all ingredients: (Set aside 2 tbsp of ketchup.) Ground beef, milk, egg, bread crumbs, onion, green pepper, ketchup, salt and sugar. Mix well.
-Press into 4" x 8" ungreased load pan.
-Bake at 350 degrees for one hour.
-Remove from oven. Drizzle remaining 2 tbsp. of ketchup over top of loaf. Return to oven and bake an additional 15 minutes.

Easy Cheesy Hash Brown Casserole

Ingredients:
1 – 8 oz. container of sour cream (regular or light)
1 - 10.75 oz. can cream of chicken soup
3 – Cups shredded sharp cheddar cheese
1 – 2 lb. bag of shredded frozen hash browns (THAWED)
¾ stick melted butter
1 tsp. salt
¼ tsp. pepper

Preheat oven to 350 degrees.

Mix all ingredients. Pack ingredients into 8-1/2 x 11 glass baking dish. Bake uncovered for one hour.

*You can also add ½ cup chopped yellow onion. For less bitter taste, sauté onion and then add to mixture before baking.

**I haven't tried it but, I think bacon bits would taste great!

About The Author

Hope Callaghan is an author who loves to write Christian books, especially Christian Mystery and Cozy Mystery books. Born and raised in a small town in West Michigan, she now lives in Florida with her husband.

She is the proud mother of one daughter and a stepdaughter and stepson. When she's not doing the thing she loves best - writing books - she enjoys cooking, traveling and reading books.

Hope loves to connect with her readers!

Visit **hopecallaghan.com** for information on special offers and soon-to-be-released books!

Email: hope@hopecallaghan.com

Facebook page:
http://www.facebook.com/hopecallaghanauthor

Other Books by Author, Hope Callaghan:

DECEPTION CHRISTIAN MYSTERY SERIES:
Waves of Deception: Samantha Rite Series Book 1
Winds of Deception: Samantha Rite Series Book 2
Tides of Deception: Samantha Rite Series Book 3

GARDEN GIRLS CHRISTIAN COZY MYSTERIES SERIES:
Who Murdered Mr. Malone? Book 1 – **FREE!**
Grandkids Gone Wild: Book 2
Smoky Mountain Mystery: Book 3
Death by Dumplings: Book 4
Eye Spy: Book 5 (Book List Continued Next Page)

GARDEN GIRLS CHRISTIAN COZY MYSTERIES SERIES: (Continued)

Magnolia Mansion Mysteries: Book 6
Missing Milt: Book 7
Bully in the 'Burbs: Book 8
Fall Girl: Book 9

CRUISE SHIP CHRISTIAN COZY MYSTERIES SERIES:
Starboard Secrets Cruise Ship Cozy Mysteries Book 1
Portside Peril: Cruise Ship Cozy Mysteries Book 2
Lethal Lobster: Cruise Ship Cozy Mysteries Book 3
Deadly Deception: Cruise Ship Cozy Mysteries Book 4

SWEET SOUTHERN SLEUTHS (Short Stories):
Teepees and Trailer Parks – **FREE!**
Bag of Bones
Southern Stalker
Two Settle the Score
Sweet Southern Sleuths Box Set: Books 1-4

Made in the USA
San Bernardino, CA
10 October 2016